"You knew this was going to happen... "

His words made Fleur laugh a little wildly. "You did too, Julian, only you had a reason. Well, think again!" she went on contemptuously. "You won't destroy me as you destroyed my mother."

The long-simmering hatred she had felt for Julian had to be kept alive. It was her only protection. But Julian jerked her easily into his arms, forcibly holding her head up to him.

"Don't touch me, Julian!" Even as she spoke, her excitement grew.

"Do you think I don't know when a woman is leading me on?" His voice was deep and husky.

She gave a little cry, more seductive than she could ever know, and Julian lowered his head, not crushing her into surrender but taking her mouth with passion and a slow urgency....

Temple of Fire

by

MARGARET WAY

Harlequin Books

TORONTO • LONDON • LOS ANGELES • AMSTERDAM
SYDNEY • HAMBURG • PARIS • STOCKHOLM • ATHENS • TOKYO

Original hardcover edition published in 1980
by Mills & Boon Limited

ISBN 0-373-02429-0

Harlequin edition published September 1981

CHAPTER ONE

SHE was on the point of collapse and she knew it; stripped of control by this, the last shock. Instinctively she shut her eyes to right her rocking world and when she opened them again, he had her firmly by the arm, supporting her.

She could have wept for the outrage and indeed tears sprang to her heavily fringed eyes.

'Fleur?'

She couldn't, *wouldn't* answer him though she remembered his voice as clearly as though he had spoken to her yesterday instead of a lifetime ago.

She kept her face averted, feeling such incredulity, such antagonism, her drooping body straightened, then tensed into breakability. She had thrown a shadowy black veil over her flaming curls and against its border of fine lace her white, white skin had a shocking pallor. She could feel the anger beginning to tremble inside her and she had to try and breathe deeply to settle herself.

Of all the things she had dreaded, she had never expected this.

The minister's voice flowed on like an actor's—the frailty of life, the inevitability of death. Just at the moment, it was Fleur's private opinion he didn't even care. How dared he come here on this terrible day? She was consumed by a bleak and bitter anger. His presence was an insult, calculated by an expert. There was even a touch of contempt in the way he was holding her. It must seem he was supporting her, when in reality they both knew she was a hostage, isolated by his power.

He had always had an excess of everything— looks, virility, a rapier brain, money. . . . She could feel his eyes on her profile, searching for any flicker of emotion. Was there ever a time he had held her with great tenderness? Memories nagged at her, needling in her brain. As a small girl he had been her demi-god, so her disillusionment had been profound.

Here was a man who could have been her friend, an idol found wanting. Now she judged him with a different set of measures.

Don't touch me! It was amazing she wasn't screaming it aloud. Under that strikingly handsome exterior was a monster. Never again would she commit herself into his hands. Her mother was laid to rest now and the pain was like a naked blade to the heart. One tragedy had ended, another could never be allowed to begin.

She tried to fix her attention in a grey, forbidding world and her small face was like a cameo carved in alabaster against the sombre black veil. She wouldn't easily forgive herself for having to endure his touch. Her heart quailed at the harshness of her mother's hatred for this man. Unlike her mother, hatred made her feel sick. A compassionate Lord had taught we must all forgive one another. Would her mother forgive in her eternal silence?

A sob broke from her trembling mouth.

He seemed to hold her to him more closely, an action she couldn't survive. Whirling clouds seemed to be coming for her, divining she could stand no more, and just as the minister brought the service to a close, Fleur precipitated her own small crisis and fainted.

When she became fully aware again, she was half lying in his arms. They were in the back seat of a chauffeur-driven, luxuriously fitted Silver Shadow that was gliding powerfully away from the place where her mother had been lain to rest for ever.

'How are you now?'

She refused to believe he cared, though the intentness of his gaze troubled her. There was a special vice to deeply blue eyes, they promised trust even as they betrayed.

In her mind she withdrew sharply, but her body was too weak to move. 'I can't believe you're here.' The effort of saying it left her breathless.

'I've never ceased to worry about you, Fleur.'

'Oh God!' she gave a soft, broken little laugh. Never again in her life would she yield to his terrible temptation. Her mother's experience had destroyed her faith in him for life. 'Let me up!'

'No.' He held her implacably. 'Lie quietly, child. I know exactly how you feel.'

'Then you'll know I have no illusions about you whatever!' she whispered, and her green eyes glittered feverishly.

'That's why I'm here, Fleur,' he said sombrely. 'To wipe out the past.'

'How touching!' The tears sprang to her eyes at his brutality. 'We'll write off the past eight years.'

'You haven't changed.' He touched her pale cheek with one finger. 'Still the same little Fleur—blind, because you were made blind.'

'Is it today you plan to turn me against my mother?' She struggled to draw away from him though it cost her a violent effort.

'I'm not going to allow you to inherit her bitterness.' He turned his dark head to look at her, his aura compounded of a ruthless arrogance and the dangerous magnetism that had always fascinated her.

'And how will you do *that*?' she asked brokenly. 'Who could ever forgive you?'

'For what?' He took her small hands and held them. 'Tell me, little one, what *is* it I did that turned me into a monster?'

'I want no part of you,' she whispered, and it was true. 'For the past eight years I've been punished by your misdeeds. You see, my mother detested you!'

'*Did* she?' he asked with deadly gravity. 'How can you be sure of that?'

'She hated you as I do!'

'No, Fleur.' His grasp tightened. 'You're all light where there were dark places in her soul.'

'She was beautiful!' It was impossible to break away.

'Yet she created so much ugliness.'

'I've just buried her today,' she whispered.

'Forgive me.' He looked down at their joined hands bleakly. 'I've come to ask you, Fleur, to come back to Waverley.'

'Never!' She was profoundly shocked. 'Does a man like you ask for absolution?'

'In point of fact, we all do,' he said wearily. 'Don't be afraid of me, Fleur. It is not—has never been—my intention to hurt you.'

'Yet you used your power to crush my mother. I know all about the way you treated her after your brother died, how you turned your family against her, how you made it impossible for her to stay on at Waverley. She told me all about the terrible quarrel you had before she fled.'

'Don't you want to see your brother?' he asked.

'You heartless brute!' She put out her hand convulsively as though to ward him off. 'Don't you know the terrible thing you did to Matthew and me? I had a little brother, a stepbrother—someone of my own. . . .' Her distress was so intense, she couldn't continue. Tears welled into her eyes and ran down her face.

'Here.' He took an immaculate handkerchief out of his breast pocket and handed it to her.

'I don't want the damned thing!' Angrily she pushed his hand away, brushing the tears off her face with the back of her hand. 'No one knows the pain I've suffered growing up without my brother.'

'That's not true, Fleur, even if I know it's not the right moment to say it. We couldn't let Matthew go. He's a Standford, my brother's only child. Much as it grieved us, we had no rights over you.'

'You mean you didn't want another man's child!' she corrected him bitterly. 'Well, I'm *glad* I don't have any Standford blood!'

'As it happens so am I.' He turned his dark head and his brilliant gaze raced over her; the blazing small face, the column of her throat, down to her small breasts. Her heart was beating so violently it was disturbing the thin black material of her bodice.

In a second some new element had been introduced into their fraught relationship and she moistened her suddenly dry mouth. 'I haven't seen Matthew since he was six years old.'

'Then don't you long to be reunited?'

'And where is he today, with his mother dead?' she asked, and the fluctuating colour died right away from her flawless white skin.

'We haven't told him yet, Fleur. It would have been too painful. Things haven't been easy for Matthew, as they haven't been easy for you.'

'And whose fault was that?' Her pretty voice went hard with contempt. 'You deliberately kept two innocent children apart. You did a more terrible thing to my mother and you didn't even stop to think how deeply it would affect us all. I can never forgive you!'

'I'm sure you would, if you only knew.'

'And you're ready to tell me.' She gave a brittle laugh. 'Why not? My mother's dead. She can't deny any of it.'

'She never gave us the chance!' he said coldly. 'That we never saw you again nearly broke my grandmother's heart. You were an enchanting child.'

'You mean you remember?' Her green eyes went wide with mockery. Out of duty to her mother she had deliberately repressed her memories of his grandmother, but now they came rushing back to her . . . the way Grandma Standford loved to curl her hair around her fingers. She had always had a short, silky mop. She could even feel now the warm, loving touch. In all the time she had been at Waverley she had never known anything else but loving kindness from Sarah Standford.

'When I read that she'd died, I locked myself in my room and cried.' Later her mother had come and pounded on the door, furious that Fleur had done such a thing.

'And she remembered you, Fleur.'

'Did she?' She laughed dismally.

'She even made provision for you in her will. Your mother was informed.'

'Whatever she was informed, she didn't tell me.'

He merely nodded. 'Well, it's quite safe.'

'In *your* hands?'

'Your mother did a job on you, didn't she?' he said sombrely. 'I suppose it had to be so.'

'In which case wouldn't it have been better never to come here? My mother said you were a cruel man.'

'Is that why you used to run to me as a child?'

'Children know no better.' She was disconcerted

by the images that flashed through her mind.

'Children know very well who care about them. Don't let your mother's obsession ruin your whole life. Perhaps her condition affected her behaviour.'

'So you've already asked? Yes, she died of a brain tumour, but she was always the same.'

'Then you know she liked to see people miserable.'

'*Shut up!*' Fleur had her teeth so tightly clenched her jawline was rigid.

'Do you think I want to say these things?' His tone bit into her. 'I *have* to. Burying the facts won't get us anywhere and they won't help you. Helena was a strange woman—over-emotional, irrational, and never very strong. We wanted only to protect her, but she made that impossible.'

'Oh, my God!' She tried to laugh, but it came out like the shrill little sound of a stricken bird. 'Stop talking, stop talking, you're a stranger to me now. My own little brother is a stranger, and I couldn't care less.'

'*Hush!*' He got his hand under her chin and held her face still. 'We'll go somewhere quiet and talk. We need to, little one, you must see that?'

A teardrop fell on his hand and they both seemed to look at it, the living, quivering symbol of grief.

'Please let me go.' His touch was unnerving her dreadfully. To be so close to him after all this time. . . .

'Try to relax,' he told her. 'You're not strong enough to do anything else.'

'You're wrong! I *am* strong!' she said with all the Celtic fire that was in her.

'You always were a funny, proud little thing.' He still held her, examining every inch of her face.

Was there a taunt in his velvety dark voice? She couldn't tell. Now that she really allowed herself to look at him she saw he was indeed older; a strikingly handsome, mature man. Now her scrutiny seemed to be as intense as his own. He looked what he was, a man of position and power. There was strength behind his extraordinary good looks—ruthlessness, she preferred to call it—that gave vigour to the chiselled features. His eyes contrasted starkly with black hair and black strongly marked brows and his darkly tanned skin. He was still the handsomest man she had ever seen.

'Well?' he asked gently.

'You have a cruel mouth.' Why did she say it, when it was so beautifully shaped?

'*You* haven't.'

Just the way he said it made her blink several times. As a child she had been intensely attracted to his radiance, now she saw it for what it was; a dazzling sexuality that repelled her. Men like that could only wound a woman.

'There's no place for me in your life,' she told him curtly. 'There never really was and there certainly never will be. I've done all my crying about Matthew. Perhaps I'll cry to my dying day, but you won't know about it. He's a Standford, he'll survive.'

'There's more to life than survival.'

'It would do Matthew no good for me to see him—put in a brief appearance, then disappear again. I could never hurt him like that. He was too little to really remember me anyway.'

'You don't believe that.' He frowned and his black brows drew together.

'I'm afraid to believe it. The hurt can't go on— I've had too much of it.' Her involuntary disclosure made her ashamed. It was so disloyal to the strange, unhappy woman who had been her mother.

'My grandfather wants you to come,' he told her.

'The first twinge of conscience?' she burst out in a sickened rage. 'Anything Sir Charles wants he gets. The master manipulator!'

'*Stop* that!'

For an instant she thought he was going to strike her and her whole body went rigid anticipating the blow.

'You little fool!' His eyes flashed, coldly brilliant, and the beautiful mouth set in a cruel slant. 'Did you think I was going to hit you? Five feet two of nothing with green eyes like glass?'

'I've lived too long hearing what you were like.'

'Perhaps you should start to question it.' His gleaming eyes kept her pinned.

'What purpose would it serve?' She turned her head away almost violently, staring out of the window. 'When I saw you walking towards me I was nearly shocked out of my mind. Once I trusted you. I never want to make that mistake again.'

'I'm not asking anything for myself.' He shrugged imperceptibly. 'Hate me all you like. It's Matthew who needs you.'

'How?' she cried, moved and deeply wary. 'How could the great-grandson of one of the wealthiest men in the country want *me*?'

'All the money in the world can't buy love, or break a blood tie. There was always a deep bond between you and Matt. Though you were only six years older, you mothered him. He always ran to you for love and comfort, not his mother. A very few women have no maternal feeling, and Helena was one of them.'

'You did your best to show her in that light.'

'It was quite true,' he said bleakly. 'You know that as well as I do. We had no difficulty getting custody of Matthew.'

'And why would you?' she whispered brokenly. 'A family like yours finds it easy to crush people. My mother had nothing, you had millions.'

'Don't you find it remarkable you've lived so well?' he turned on her brutally.

'How can you say that?' she asked painfully. 'We've lived quietly—very quietly. There was no money to send me on to university.'

'There was money,' he said deliberately. 'Money that was to be used *for* you and *on* you.'

'Not from you?' She had the mad desire to wrench open the door and jump out on to the freeway. She didn't want to hear his lying revelations.

'I said we had no difficulty getting custody of

Matthew. I didn't say we had to pay for it.'

'You liar!' she gasped, then choked, and in a blaze of anger threw up her hand to strike him.

'You see?' he caught her hand and nearly paralysed it, 'you know nothing about the whole tragic situation, but your solicitor will tell you you've been left very comfortably off indeed. That's if Helena did, in fact, leave it to you.'

'Standford money?' she asked with low vehemence.

'It's kept you secretly for the past eight years. Maybe you haven't noticed people don't live in houses as nice as yours?' he asked coolly.

'As your brother's widow my mother was entitled to a great deal, but she told me and I believed her that she refused to touch a penny. It was all for Matthew, the son you deprived her of.'

Anger and arrogance flared into his face. 'You're right about one thing, the money *was* for Matthew.'

'Why have you come after me?' Fleur gave a strange little laugh. 'You hated my mother, you've done everything in your power to malign her, you're still doing it, at the same time appealing to *me*. I want no part of you!'

'I'm afraid, Fleur, you're going to do what you're told!' His hand closed under her chin and he held her face up to him. 'There are debts to be paid and you're going to pay them. Matthew has never ceased to miss you. He's a solitary child, a lot like my brother.'

'Solitary?' She tilted her head away, although he

was hurting her. 'He was an adorable little boy, full of life.'

'He's badly asthmatic,' he told her bluntly. 'The doctors have told us the problem is emotional.'

'And you can't stand it, can you?' she asked feverishly. 'Standfords demand perfection. My poor little Matt, he's flawed, is he? The only reason your brother married my mother was because she was beautiful. He didn't want her when he found out she had poor health.'

'She told you that?' He looked at her, his handsome face impassive.

'Does it really matter now?' For the first time Fleur seemed completely aware of her surroundings. The city was crowded and people were turning to stare at the chauffeur-driven Rolls. She was even bitterly amused that the driver hadn't heard one word, safely shut off from them by the glass partition. It would be necessary, she thought, otherwise employees might start selling secrets.

'Where do you think you're taking me?' she asked wearily.

'To my hotel. It doesn't suit me to drive around in the car for ever.'

'What a ghastly day!' She deliberately relaxed her back against the deep plush upholstery, willing herself to gather up her resources. She hadn't the slightest intention of going anywhere further with him. She had to be by herself to think. Her darling little Matt, an asthmatic? Why, in six years she doubted if he had ever even had a cold. All kinds of jumbled plans were running through her head.

If Matt really wanted her, why couldn't they live together? She would have no hesitation using Standford money on the rightful heir. It took her a moment to see the bitter irony in the fact that she had accepted what he had told her and she shook her head hopelessly. What a day to think her mother too had lied!

The Rolls was gliding into the loading zone outside the city's leading hotel and she saw the smartly uniformed doorman make his way briskly towards them. Now was her chance. Julian Standford had his head turned away from her, and in a flash she opened up the offside door and sprang out.

To the startled onlookers it seemed like a good way to get killed, but for the agitated Fleur it was salvation. With the heavy traffic slowed by pedestrians moving out into the crossing, she made her frantic, illegal dash.

'You silly girl!' an elderly lady said to her wrathfully. 'You young people have no respect for regulations!'

'Haven't you heard of desperation?' Fleur turned her wide eyes on the woman's face, seeing the indignation give way to a puzzled concern. She must have looked a sight with her white face and her black dress, dashing madly away from the parked Rolls. On today of all days she had worn no lipstick on her tenderly moulded mouth and the only colour about her was the titian of her hair and her leaf-green eyes.

Like a miracle no policeman came forward to take her to task and she hurried into a department store, knowing there was a taxi rank at the other side. He wouldn't make any attempt to follow her. It would only add to the intrigue. His name, even his face was well known to the general public. It was always the way when one was heir to a mining empire.

Her heart was beating very fast, but she never once looked back. One day she had always told herself she would see Matt again. She had kept his six-year-old image burning brightly in her mind. Her most deeply treasured private possession. Her mother had called him a Standford and dismissed him from her mind, but Fleur had known that was only because of the terrible pain. To separate a child from his mother—what suffering!

Faces seemed to be alert on her, a white-skinned redhead in the sort of black dress that said funeral. A big man with a beard knocked into her and apologised, then resumed his way through the crowd. At least he distracted some attention from her because he was very flamboyantly dressed.

She was breathless by the time she reached the street and within sight of the taxi rank. Thank God there was a line-up! She almost flung herself at the first car and just as she put her hand out to open the back door, a man's hand came down forcefully on the slender bones of her shoulder.

'Get in,' he said tonelessly.

Now, looking back at him, she saw she had better obey.

'Where to, sir?' the driver turned to them.

'Windsor Park,' Julian Standford said abruptly. 'One-two-one Skyline Drive.'

Fleur's anger flared again, though she was shaking like a leaf. 'You've gone too far!'

'Let's not talk about it,' he returned curtly. 'I would have expected a greater sense of self-preservation from you.'

'Look, I'm here!' she risked saying with a terrible banter.

He immediately transferred his attention to out of the window. Heated discussions in a taxi weren't his style.

In complete silence they made the twenty-minute drive to the garden suburb while the taxi driver kept casting surreptitious little glances into his rear vision mirror. There was a lot of drama in driving a taxi and he suspected the minute they got out there would be a terrible fight. Both of his passengers looked tense and strained, locked together in a silent passion. The man's face teased his memory, but it wasn't until they got out he remembered who the man was—the mining guy, the millionaire.

Now they were in the house, the shadow of Helena came relentlessly between them. There was a portrait of her over the fireplace in the living room and Julian Standford went to stand before it.

'I keep remembering how beautiful she was when David first brought her to the house.'

Fleur made a sound of distress and came to stand at his side. He was very tall and she felt small and beaten. Her mother had had the darkest, deepest eyes she had ever seen. Now they looked down on them both with a curious lifelike glitter. She was wearing a red chiffon evening dress and her beauty was breathtaking.

'It's wrong for you to be here,' said Fleur, but Julian did not reply. He didn't even seem to be aware of her staring up at the masterly executed painting. Superb as it was, Fleur had never liked it. It pointed up the strangeness in Helena, the kind of secret gloating. The smile on the lovely mouth was slow and vaguely scornful and in the depths of those fathomless eyes was a wicked triumph. It had been painted in the early months of her second marriage, and even then she had been very young.

Julian drew a long breath and released it wearily. 'Everything she touched she damaged. My brother, irreparably.'

'You can't mean what you're saying!'

'David loved her, but she had no pity on him.'

'Please stop,' she said frantically. 'Let her rest.'

'I'm sorry, Fleur,' he turned to her at last. 'It's been hell on you.'

'Oh, spare me!' She moved away, putting distance between them. 'You can't do anything to either of us any more.'

'You're overwrought,' he said quietly. 'Why don't you sit down?'

'I will when you leave.' She had to turn away from the sight and sound of him. There was only menace in the ruthless charm.

'*Please*, Fleur.' He came behind her and held her by the shoulders. 'Don't let the past keep on hurting you. You're so young.' He slid his fingers down her bare arms and she turned her head.

'It must be an odd feeling for you meeting with resistance?'

'My concern is for Matthew. I'm asking you, *begging* you to come back to him as his sister.'

'It's too late!' Her agitation was transparent and he drew her towards him a little roughly.

'Then what shall I tell him? You won't come.'

'He doesn't even know I'm here.'

'He will soon. You were photographed in your mad dash across the street.'

'What?' She froze with shock.

'The press think they're entitled to follow me around. Most of the time we're pretty pally, but I have a feeling we're not going to be able to cover up your little folly. To anyone looking it certainly looked as if there was a story.'

'*Stories*,' she corrected him scornfully. 'Hundreds of stories about you.'

'Not a one of them that wasn't passed on.' He gave a short, humourless laugh. 'We can't really be told anything, Fleur, unless we want to be told. You've found it too easy to believe every accusation. It's a good deal more difficult discovering the truth, and sometimes it's better not to reveal it at all. I'm appealing to you as the compassionate little creature I remember. Come back to Waverley. There's nothing there to make you afraid.'

Longing struck her like a physical pain ... the eternal summer of Waverley ... Matthew, laughing, running after her in the dancing sunlight. Even as a baby he had been physically all Standford. That meant he would be handsome and at fourteen probably a lot taller than she was. All the Standford men were tall and superbly athletic, yet Matt was asthmatic. It upset her when she knew how alarming that condition could be. One of the girls in her senior year at school had been a chronic asthmatic. It had been sobering watching her struggle for her very breath and she had been terrified of misplacing her atomiser, dependent on it really, as though to be without it provoked an attack. She remembered, too, one of the teachers had been very short with the girl as though if she only tried, she could cure herself. Emotional, Louise, the teacher used to cry. Not an allergy. Focus all your attention on getting better.

In spite of the fierce tension between them, Julian was still holding her by the arms. 'What are you thinking about?'

'The agony of asthma. The torture of just trying to breathe. The things we take for granted.'

He looked down at her glowing head. 'I know just having you back with him will help Matthew. He's waited for eight years.'

'You're using me, aren't you?' She fixed her great eyes on his face. 'But at least Matthew is important to you.'

'Then you'll come?' A kind of exultation lay on him like a patina of light, and she clenched a small fist and hit it into his chest.

'I don't know. I've got to *think*!'

'You know in your heart you want to come.'

The faint tenderness in his voice haunted her. She remembered it from so long ago. 'I'd sacrifice anything if I thought it would help Matthew.'

'I'm convinced that it will. All of us are.'

'But then you're the sort of man who's always convinced of the rightness of his decisions,' she said with fresh anger. 'Who caused this dilemma in the first place? I must never forget that.'

'So you've been lonely,' he released her abruptly and went to stand before the portrait again. 'So has Matthew, and he's not as spirited as you. No one, even your mother, meant things to happen, they just did.'

'You never approved of her.' Because she was shaking she had to drop into a chair.

'No. I knew from the beginning what she would do to my brother.'

'What *did* she do?' Fleur stood up again in her agitation, a small, too slender girl with a delicate, patrician face. 'I was only a child, but I'll never forget the way he used to look at her.'

'Did she ever look at him the same way?' He turned around to her and though his dark face was unmoving, she knew he was furiously angry.

'Why, I . . . ' She looked at him with terrified eyes. 'What are you trying to say? All your damnable accusations!'

At the sob in her voice, all his anger seemed to spend itself. 'No matter what she *said*, she never brought herself to destroy the portrait.'

'But it's magnificent!' Fleur looked up at her mother in the heavy, gilded frame.

'And it tells you all you ever needed to know about Helena.'

The starkness of his tone stripped her of her expected indignation. Now suddenly she sensed some devastating truths her mother had always kept from her. Stepping back in time was too painful a process and though she had retained a clear picture of Julian, her memory of her stepfather, Julian's elder brother, was surprisingly hazy. She could remember he was like Julian but without the dangerous attraction, the high-mettled determined look that was so like the tyrannical old man who had made the family fortune. Her mother had made her swear she would never go near the Standfords. They were a brood of vipers who ruined everything they touched.

What should she do? How should she choose; for her mother or Matthew? There had been enough tragedies at Waverley. She didn't think she could bear to find out the hidden ones.

'I don't know,' she said aloud into the fraught silence. 'My mother would never let me do this.'

'But we have only ourselves to live with,' he told her. 'How could you turn your back on Matthew and be free of that memory? The last thing he ever wanted was to lose you.'

'Put like that, you give me no choice.' The green eyes she fixed on him were filled with a passionate longing. 'I don't even understand myself. My mother found anger and enmity at Waverley, mightn't I find the same?'

'You're nothing like your mother,' he said harshly, and his brilliant blue eyes explored every fine contour of her face. 'Besides, you were pretty happy at Waverley as a child. Surely the good times sometimes come back to haunt you?'

'I remember how you used to call me Flower Face.'

'And you still look the same.' He smiled faintly and there was a dark magic in the way his mouth curved. 'I don't want you to stay here. There's nothing in this house but pain.'

She couldn't deny it, face to face with the facts. Still she flushed and refused to bend to his strong will. 'I'll be perfectly all right.'

'Please allow me my concern, Fleur,' his glance struck her averted profile. 'You shouldn't be alone.'

'Then what is it you want me to do?' She threw up her head helplessly.

'Just come with me and shut the door.'

'I can't. Not yet.' She held a hand to the pulsing vein in her throat. 'I have a job, the house, lots of things to be considered.'

'I can attend to all that.'

'I'm sure you can!' she answered him, and her tone wasn't kind. 'What will you do, dispose of everything so I have nowhere to come back to?'

'You can have anything you want,' he said, and his blue eyes glittered under the lids. 'We don't want you to come for a month or a year. When you come back to Waverley, you come back as family.'

'I'm afraid!' Her softly impassioned voice betrayed her agitation. 'How can I be sure I can even help Matthew? You could be lying to me now!'

He came to stand in front of her and looked down at her with a look of brooding concentration. 'For God's sake, Fleur, let go. We've got to salvage something from this mess.'

The hotness of tears scorched her eyes and she stood torn and confused with the light glinting on her short, silky curls.

'Look at me, Fleur.' He took her by the shoulders, infinitely practised in the art of persuasion. 'I was never your enemy.'

'But you let me go.' A child's pain revealed itself in her broken sigh.

'Do you imagine I had any choice?' He said it sharply and his strong fingers bruised. 'Your mother wasn't going to leave us you.'

'That's exactly what any mother would do!' Anger shook her voice. 'You took her son from her and the pain nearly drove her insane.'

'All right!' He gave her a terrible, cynical glance. 'Naturally you must believe that. Never mind, I'll stay the monster, but we're both trying to work out something for Matthew. Whatever life is, it isn't easy. You can hate and resent me if you have to, but I'm taking you home to your brother.'

Tears sprang from her eyes, blurred his face, the room, the big portrait of her mother. She had always believed she and Matthew would be together again; she had counted on it. She nodded her head and in the end went back with him to Waverley. It was what she had always wanted, but for a long time the wish remained buried with her mother.

CHAPTER TWO

OUTSIDE the airport building the sunlight was blinding.

'This way, Fleur,' said Julian, and took her arm.

From somewhere close by, a flashlight went off, then another. She winced and went to turn, but he kept on moving her briskly forward. 'Don't look around.' His voice was very formal, overlaid with ironic tones.

'Mr Standford?'

A small wiry man rushed up and Julian gave him a thin smile. 'Not now, Bob.'

'Back to business, then?'

'When I have a bit of news I shall deliver it to you. *Privately*.'

'Got ya!' The man made a gesture that came close to a salute, all the while examining Fleur out of the corner of his eyes.

'Getting caught in an airport is like being under siege,' added Julian.

'The price of fame, the little man offered jauntily, and went off apparently quite happy.

'Who was that?' Fleur lapsed into curiosity.

'Bob Garrity, one of our best journalists. He's always there when he scents a story.'

'I see.' Fleur fell silent abruptly. There had been a very illuminating photograph of her on the front page of the *Sydney Morning Herald*. Attention fixed itself on the very rich and everyone who surrounded them.

A porter followed them up, wheeling their luggage. She had somehow expected another Rolls, and there it was, with the uniformed driver standing outside waiting alertly for their appearance.

'Good, there's Adams.' Julian said it very calmly without a touch of arrogance. He was accustomed to being picked up at airports by Rolls-Royces, but Fleur found it almost staggering.

'Good afternoon, sir,' the driver said to him with a smile. 'Miss.' He tipped his hat respectfully.

'Would you please get the things in for us, Des.'

'Right away, sir.'

Of course he would jump. Everyone jumped, and he didn't seem to care.

This time the Rolls was a different colour and there was no glass partition inside. When they were all in the car, Julian introduced the driver to her and he gave her a straightforward, guileless smile. 'Welcome home, miss.'

'Is my grandfather at home?' Julian asked.

'I ran him into the city for a meeting with the premier. That was at ten o'clock. I know he wasn't expecting you home this afternoon.'

'We finished our business a little earlier,' Julian explained.

'Young Matt is so excited, I think he'll explode.'

'I feel the same way,' Fleur told him a little shakily, though it wasn't strictly true. Her excitement was overlaid by a physical and mental exhaustion.

The six weeks preceeding her mother's death had almost extinguished her strength—the terrible consultations, the tests, the brain scan that had shown up the tumour. She couldn't cry in the daytime now, but at night she knew her pillow would be wet.

Julian must have taken note of her expression, for his lean, long-fingered hand covered her own. 'You're going to be happy, Fleur.'

'God knows,' she sighed.

The drive was a long one, but at last they turned into the long, curved driveway which she now remembered as clearly as though she had turned into it yesterday. It was the early days of December and the four acres that surrounded the house were ablaze with colour. An avenue of jacarandas led up to the mansion and the flowering miracles of the tropics, the poincianas, were given all the space that they needed. They filled the park-like grounds with their sumptuous colour and their beautiful lacy branches threw shadows on the ground.

Up ahead stood the house; no different from what it had been all those years ago. Ivy sheened the rosy brickwork with green and birds winged in to the high Tudor gables.

'It's no different,' she said huskily. 'Only we have changed.'

'Don't be bitter, Fleur,' he begged.

'*Please!* I'm doing the best I can.'

They were approaching the front of the house, and she felt her eyes widen in a stare. A boy had run down the stone steps and emotion hit her in such a rush she gave an incoherent little cry.

'Pull up, Des,' Julian said—almost un-
necessarily, because both men had been moved to
instant pity. The chauffeur swung the big car
effortlessly off the gravel and the instant he had
stopped Fleur threw open the door and started
running.

She didn't need to wonder if this was really
Matthew, her every intuition told her so. The
intensity of her feelings, like spring after winter,
were shared by the boy. His eyes glazed with
wonder and though his heart was hammering and
his breath came almost painfully he too was im-
pelled into flight.

'God, it would make you cry!' the chauffeur said
softly, and only a few yards away brother and
sister came together.

'Matt,' said Fleur on a caught breath. *'Matthew!'*

He was much taller than she was and impossibly
thin, but his eyes were the same. 'I thought you'd
never come.' The thin, boy's arms gripped like
iron.

'I'm here, really here.' She heard the terrible,
rasping breath. He looked beautiful to her, but so
pitifully frail that the crushing guilt she had felt on
her mother's account fell away from her. 'We'll
always have one another from now on.'

'Matthew.' Julian Standford came towards
them, put out his hands and touched both of their
heads.

'I can hardly believe it!' Matthew's blue eyes

were great pools of light. 'Thanks, Uncle Julian. Grandad told me you'd gone to find Fleur and now that you've found her, she's never going away again.'

With their arms twisted around each other, they walked up to the house. There was a storm of emotion inside both of them, a sadness in the fact that their mother was dead, and a blissful happiness at finding each other again.

In the cool formality of the entrance hall a woman greeted them, her narrowed, measuring glance on both of their faces. 'So you've come back to us, Fleur!'

'Aunt Charlotte.' Fleur went forward, by no means welcomed or reassured by Charlotte Standford's presence. Charlotte didn't smile or make any attempt to, but as Fleur drew close, she dropped a conventional kiss on the girl's cheek. 'Let me look at you. You must be nineteen now.'

'I feel years older.' Unlike the Standford men, though there was the stamp of elegance about her, Charlotte missed out on their splendid good looks. And their charm.

'We all have our bitter little facts to swallow,' she returned soberly, then looked at the brilliant-eyed boy. 'You mustn't become over-excited, Matthew. You know it's bad for you.'

'On this occasion it could only be good for him,' Julian told his eldest sister a little curtly. 'I'm sure you'll want to show Fleur her room. She's been travelling since early morning. I had to make a stop-over in Sydney.'

'Of course you're right, Julian,' a little colour came into Charlotte's fine olive skin. 'Come up, my dear. We've given you your old room. There wasn't time to redecorate it, but you may do so if you wish.'

'*Let's!*' Matthew took his sister's hand in a deeply loving gesture. 'Grandfather wants me to be an engineer like him and Uncle Julian when it's time to go to university, but I want to be an architect. I love houses, don't you?'

'Especially when they're as beautiful as this one,' Fleur smiled at him.

Charlotte shook her head. 'Don't go encouraging him to study architecture, Fleur. All the Standford men are engineers. It's necessary for the business.'

'To some extent, yes,' Julian Standford agreed, 'but I'm sure we can fit in an architect or two.'

'You know what Grandfather expects,' Charlotte paused on the winding staircase and looked down at her brother. 'You've been the only one to oppose him.'

To Fleur's eyes it sounded more like an accusation than praise.

'I've told the boy he can make his own choice,' Julian said evenly, and took a few steps away from them. 'I have to make a few phone calls, then I'm going out.'

'I wish you'd speak to Grandfather,' Charlotte seemed to beg him.

'Matt,' Julian addressed his nephew, 'you know the way, show Fleur up.'

Charlotte looked at the boy and nodded, then she walked back down the stairs to where her brother was standing. There seemed to be some pressure or tension on her, and Fleur pressed Matthew's hand and together they continued on their way.

'Lottie has to ask Uncle Julian everything,' Matthew confided. 'I think she should have got married and had a home of her own, then she wouldn't have to ask anyone anything.'

'I don't think it's ever as easy as that,' Fleur said lightly. 'Sir Charles, how is he?'

'Marvellous, really,' Matthew said. 'It's just he's so set in his ways. When you're important and you've got such a lot of money people don't seem to do anything but agree with you.'

'Except Uncle Julian,' Fleur supplied dryly.

'That's different!' Matthew looked at her and smiled. 'Uncle Julian is splendid. He could come face to face with the devil and make him back off.'

From the light in her stepbrother's eyes, Fleur could see he idolised his uncle, but she felt a frightening wave of antagonism wash over her. Like his grandfather, Julian Standford was made in the same infinitely arrogant mould. People like that might found empires, but they weren't men to mate with or call family. She had learned that the hard way, and the bitterness would always linger.

'Are you tired? Would you like something to eat?' Matthew enquired solicitously.

'I'm too bursting with happiness,' she said, a little emotionally.

'I know.' Matthew squeezed her fingers hard. 'Grandfather told me, but I wasn't going to believe it until I saw you with my own eyes.'

'Have I changed?' They had paused at an open doorway and Fleur turned to look at him.

'I never expected you to, and you haven't!' Matthew's eyes brushed her glowing hair and her lovely young face. 'I've forgotten my mother. Is that terrible of me?'

'You were only a little boy,' Fleur said softly.

'Anyway, she never wanted me.' Matthew's thin shoulders moved in a shrug.

'Who told you that?' Fleur was shocked by the starkness of his tone.

'Why, Lottie,' said Matthew.

'Even if she was harming you by saying it?' Fleur felt that quick rush of anger again.

'It doesn't matter, Fleur. Really it doesn't.' Matthew recognised the flash in her eyes. 'I'm sorry she's dead, but I find it hard to care. If she really wanted me, she could have put up a fight.'

'But, darling,' Fleur grasped his bony wrist, 'who could fight a man as rich and powerful as Sir Charles? Mother loved you. She just couldn't have you, that's all.'

'Lottie said she was a strange woman and it was a good thing neither of us had taken after her.'

'She had no right!'

'She's looked after me ever since you went.' Matthew's thin arm encircled his sister's shoulders. 'Don't let's get upset. You're here now.'

'Of course.' Fleur smiled at him, the green eyes

revealing an enormous tenderness. 'Now let's see
what we're going to do about my room!'

When Charlotte joined them five or six minutes
later, Fleur was sitting on the bed and Matthew
was moving around the room with both arms up.
There was a flush on his skin and his gentle, rather
hesitant voice had firmed into a boyish authority.

'Of course you can get a decorator if you like,
but I think we can do it just as well ourselves,
probably better. The walls would be super covered
with a very soft, metallic paper—silver-grey like a
pearl with perhaps a green flower. You have a
wonderful view across the garden, so I'd pull all
those curtains down and have shutters that fold
back. There's too much clutter in here too.'

'Actually there are some very good antiques and
good pictures,' Charlotte said. 'It won't do at all
for you to get too carried away, Matthew. You
know Grandfather sees the bill for everything.'

'Really it's perfectly all right as it is,' Fleur
intervened a little coolly. Who had mentioned
making changes in the first place anyway?

'Of course it isn't!' Matthew frowned and for
the first time sounded like a Standford. 'We're
going to do everything we can to make you happy
and comfortable. Hang the expense! That's what
Uncle Julian always says.'

'That's all very well for him,' Charlotte replied a
little dryly, 'but Grandfather takes a different line
with me.'

'And one of the reasons is because he's made
you his slave,' Matthew supplied unexpectedly.

'Don't be ridiculous, Matthew!' Charlotte said sharply.

'I'm sorry, Lottie, it's true!' Matthew insisted. 'The nicer you are to him, the more growly he gets. Sheena calls him the old tyrant.'

'Really, Matthew!' Charlotte said warningly, and cast a glance towards Fleur, still seated on the bed.

'Sheena's Uncle Julian's latest girl-friend,' Matthew explained to his stepsister confidingly. 'She's lasted the longest too. I don't like her much.'

'You know very well she's a lovely girl,' Charlotte said. 'Grandfather likes her and she's not likely to call him an old tyrant to his face.'

'I expect he'd like it!' said Matthew. 'The funny thing about him, he likes people who stand up to him. I can't do it very well, neither can Lottie. He might be an old man, but he's still pretty fierce.'

'I'm sure he's been very good to you, Matthew,' Charlotte said reprovingly, 'so let's hear no more. Fleur, would you like something to eat? We don't have dinner until eight o'clock.'

'I'd love a cup of coffee!' Fleur slid gracefully off the bed. 'Where are my things, Aunt Charlotte? I'll put them away.'

'Don't bother, dear.' Charlotte waved a long, shapely hand. 'One of the girls will do it for you. We pay them well and they won't mind.'

'All right, then.' Fleur subsided, though she would rather have done it herself.

'If you're not feeling tired, perhaps you'd like to come downstairs again?' Charlotte paused at the door, unmistakably a Standford, but too tall and too formidable of feature for feminine charm.

'I will after I freshen up.' Fleur smiled at her, remembering a younger, kinder, far less intimidating Charlotte.

'Come along then, Matthew,' Charlotte ordered, and held out her hand. 'Give your sister a few minutes, then we'll all have coffee on the terrace.'

'Would you believe it, I've stopped wheezing!' Matthew exclaimed in wonderment, his head tilted to the side as he listened to his own body.

'Really?' Charlotte advanced on him, her brow knotted in concentration.

'I think so.' Matthew heaved a few, quick breaths. 'I didn't tell you, Fleur, but I have this rotten asthma.'

Charlotte sighed deeply. 'We've had him to all the specialists.'

'It's rotten!' Matthew said again, apologising for his own condition.

'And as terrible as it is,' Fleur told him, 'it's been known to go away. Just like that!'

'Nonsense, Fleur!' Charlotte's blue eyes darkened with annoyance. 'It's not a kindness to build up his hopes. He's suffered dreadfully for years now—we all have. Even Grandfather cares deeply, but no one can do anything about it.'

'Perhaps he's been in a chronic anxiety state,' said Fleur, and took her brother's hand. 'After all, the mind has tremendous control over the body. He was wheezing badly when I arrived, now he hasn't had time to think about it.'

'If it were only that easy!' Charlotte's expression softened magically as she looked down at her nephew's face. 'David had a few passing problems as a boy. He never had Julian's wonderful health and vigour. I suppose it started there.'

'Then Matthew should take up some sport. Swimming,' Fleur suggested.

'I get infections,' Matthew shook his head gloomily. 'Uncle Julian even had the pool converted to salt, but I'm always coming down with something.'

'Then skating,' Fleur began.

'I suppose I'll break a leg.'

'And I can't say I want that,' Charlotte said firmly. 'By the same token I'm convinced this asthma will go away—in time. I never cease to pray about it.'

'Meantime I'd try the ocean,' said Fleur. 'Hasn't Queensland got the most beautiful beaches of all?'

'Quite,' Charlotte agreed, and got her hand on Matthew's shoulder. 'We'll talk about this again, Fleur. I guess you can't know everything we've tried.'

Fleur accepted the reproof and Matthew's understanding half smile. Still as they went down the hallway, she heard him say to his aunt:

'I'm certain no one said *skating*!'

For the rest of the afternoon brother and sister didn't waste a moment. Hand in hand they walked all over the house and the garden, with so much to say to one another it was like a wonderful trip of discovery. The colour hadn't faded from Matthew's cheeks and his breathing was still normal.

'All those letters I wrote to you,' he said, 'and you never got them.'

'Mother must have made the decision that they would only hurt me more.'

'At least it's possible to start afresh,' Matthew said happily. 'It's like a dream having you here.'

'And you really want to be an architect?' Fleur looked intently into his Standford blue eyes.

'I do, but Grandfather frightens the hell out of me sometimes. How could I ever tell him?'

'You've obviously told your uncle and aunt.'

Matthew bent and picked up a pebble, then sent it skimming across the man-made lake that was glinting a shining silver. 'Well, Lottie would never tell on me, she's extra protective, and Uncle Julian is my idol. Honestly, he's brilliant! He's got so many qualifications. I'm just glad he's around to be Grandfather's heir. I dread the thought of big business—you have to be a special kind of person. Apart from anything else, it's so strenuous. I could never cope—anyway, not with asthma.'

'Why don't we get started on a swimming programme?' Fleur suggested to him seriously.

'Poor old Lottie would have a fit. She needs a bit of peace. She's really been terribly good to me, you know, running me all over the place to doctors and sitting up nights. I've missed quite a lot of school, so it's a good thing I'm pretty smart.'

'A lot of well known athletes have suffered from asthma in their youth,' said Fleur, collapsing into a garden seat. 'The thing is to build yourself up.

We might have to cope with a few infections, though I don't see why if the pool is salt. . . .'

'Well, actually I haven't been in it all that much,' Matthew confessed. 'Especially not at exam time. I didn't want to miss out.'

'Well, now you're on holiday for two months,' Fleur pointed out to him. 'We'll swim in the pool and we'll go to the beach a lot.'

'With your red hair?' Matthew's face lightened and he tweaked at a fiery curl.

'I can cover myself with cream,' she offered cheerfully.

'Blimey, that will look funny!'

The wide smile and the glowing eyes took Fleur right back to the time they had been torn apart. Matthew, she decided, desperately needed her. *He* hadn't been lying about that.

'Now just you remember,' she said firmly, and got to her feet, 'now I'm back, I'm the boss.'

'I'd very much like to know when you weren't,' Matthew challenged.

'You're going to get better. I'm going to make it my business.'

'Don't let's tell anyone,' said Matthew. 'Lottie will only fuss, and illness makes Granddad furious. It's the one thing he's got no control over.'

'And Uncle Julian?' Fleur's eyes searched her young brother's profile.

'Let's surprise him. He's so perfect, isn't he? They still rave on about him at school. The great Julian Standford's nephew, that's all I am. As well as being a brain he must have been something of a sporting phenomenon. Needless to say I'm a write-off in that department.'

'You're too young, darling, to write yourself off,' Fleur willed her young brother to turn around to her. 'The past is behind us and the future unfurls, shining with hope and promise. You're very clever at school, which is a great blessing, and even if you don't turn into Uncle Julian by the time we're finished, you'll be able to relax and enjoy any sport that pleases you.'

'Do you really think so?' Matthew asked so wistfully that Fleur tried to lighten it with a joke.

'All except football,' she said firmly. 'All those wild spills that finish up in being strung up in pulleys.'

'Uncle Julian was very good at it.'

'*Matthew*,' Fleur began.

'All right, all right,' Matthew took her hand again, seemingly starving for loving contact. 'Uncle Julian I can't be, but I promise you, you won't be ashamed of me.'

'You can do what you damned well like and I'd never be that. Except maybe rob a bank,' Fleur added consideringly.

'Or hijack a plane. . . .'

'Or sell secrets to the other side.'

Matthew's wistfulness dissolved like mist. All the way back to the house they made a joke of it, so that nobody looking at them would ever know their lives had been deeply touched by tragedy.

Fleur heard her brother's breathing, light and even, and the first peace she had known in a long time touched her heart. What was life after all but service to the people one loved? The thought made her humble and started the thaw in her own heart. Both of them had lived through years of emotional insecurity, but time was merciful. They would heal.

It was approaching eight, and Fleur stood before the long mirror in her bedroom staring abstractedly at her own reflection. She was wearing the one and only dress she had judged suitable for the evening—indeed, for such an occasion. It was an amber slip of a dress, far from expensive, but her slight girl's body lent it surprising style. Not that she really cared about her dress with the emotions of the day churning around inside her. Now Sir Charles was back to welcome her into his home. She was very conscious of his motive, but what did it matter? Matthew was special to all of them.

He had put his head around the door more than an hour ago to tell her his grandfather—*great-grandfather*, though everyone dropped the *great*—had arrived home. Not that Fleur had needed telling. From the balcony of her room, afloat over the beautiful garden, she had seen the dark blue Rolls sweep up the drive. A few minutes later she had caught Sir Charles' tone, then Julian's, both of them damnably attractive and so terribly self-assured. There was no doubt about it, both of them possessed shattering poise and charisma. The thought almost amused her, except that she had been reared to regard them both as enemies. No matter how Matthew longed to be like Uncle Julian, she was glad he favoured his gentler, more sensitive, far less ambitious father; David, who had died so violently, so unexpectedly in a car smash. Such deaths seemed the hardest to bear. Yet had her mother mourned him?

Fleur turned away and walked to the French doors that led out on to the balcony. It was a heavenly night, the sky alive with stars. She traced the downward path through Orion, the mighty hunter's belt, to Sirius, the brightest star in the heavens. The Southern Cross was particularly bright tonight, its lowest star pointing to the Pole, a star of the first magnitude.

Such majesty! She drew a deep breath that came out as an emotional sigh. Almost at the same moment, she realised someone was looking up at her.

'Fleur?'

Light was spilling out from the ground floor and as she leaned over the balcony, Julian stepped into a brilliant triangle. 'That was a heartfelt little sigh I heard,' he said gently.

'Oh, good evening,' she answered politely.

'A bit more than *that*, I should say,' he said dryly. 'It's a very long time since I glanced up and saw you looking up at the stars. What did they tell you?'

She tilted her face upwards again. 'Oh, that I'm very small.'

'You ought to come down,' he said.

'I'm sorry, have I been keeping you waiting?'

'Grandfather is anxious to see you.'

'Then I'll come right away.'

Obviously one couldn't keep Sir Charles waiting. She didn't hurry, but moved as gently as the breeze off the balcony. Sir Charles Standford might be an extremely important man, but she had never cared and she didn't care now.

They were waiting for her in the handsome drawing room and she was vaguely aware there were strangers present.

'Ah, Fleur,' said Sir Charles, his vibrant voice cutting into the silence, 'come here and let me look at you!'

She had expected him to be much older, but he still looked the same, a proud old eagle of a man, tall and upright, with the Standford metallic blue eyes staring coolly at her.

'Good evening, Sir Charles. How very kind of you to ask me back.' She spoke her tribute with a good deal of his cool calm.

'If my son had lived, you would never have left.' He took her hands, staring at her intently, then to her surprise drew her closer and kissed her on the cheek. 'I do believe you haven't changed at all— the same little flower face, the same glorious skin and delicious curls. Please accept my sympathy in your loss.'

The last bit was a little peremptory, as though Helena's death was nobody's loss.

Julian stepped smoothly into the breach. 'Fleur,' he said gently, and held out his hand to her, 'let me introduce you to our friends.'

She had to accept his hand, irritated beyond measure with the way her skin tingled. His clasp was warm and dry, light but very strong. Probably he still had the uncanny knack of reading her mind.

Two men were moving towards her, smiling, and seated on the sofa with Charlotte was an exquisitely groomed young woman in her mid-twenties, her lustrous dark hair curving around a golden-skinned, full-lipped face. Her eyes were light brown and though the red mouth was parted in a smile the expression in the eyes was vaguely off-putting.

Her name was Sheena Lloyd. One of the men, a very pleasant and prosperous-looking business man, was her father and the other was Sir Charles' lifelong friend and personal physician Hugh Alistair.

'Of course I remember you, Dr Alistair,' Fleur shook hands in faint confusion. Though Sir Charles remained as indestructible as ever, the doctor had altered a good deal. Pounds had fallen off his once rugged frame and Fleur learned from Julian later that he had an inoperable cancer. Still his kind, wise eyes lit up with pleasure—the genuine feeling that had been so patently missing from Sheena Lloyd's dark, assessing gaze.

'Welcome back to Waverley, my dear,' he said, beaming through his gold-rimmed glasses. 'Julian tells me you've wrought a small miracle already.'

'Much too early to say, Hugh,' Charlotte murmured rather severely behind them.

'It *can* happen!' Still holding Fleur's hand, Dr Alistair looked back at Charlotte over his shoulder. 'I've been practising medicine long enough to know that.'

Obviously there was nothing wrong with his hearing.

'I don't know what gets into you sometimes, Charlotte,' Sir Charles said testily. 'I've spoken to the boy myself and he looks on top of the world.'

'Let us hope he'll remain there,' Charlotte said like the harbinger of doom.

'Would you care for something to drink before we go in to dinner, Fleur?' Julian looked down at Fleur's wonderfully glinting head.

'Thank you, no.' She didn't want to look at him, for despite everything his physical attraction was unbearable.

'Then we'll go in, shall we?' Sir Charles took Fleur's arm a shade forcefully and immediately stomped away.

'But such a surprise!' Sheena's warm, husky tones nevertheless reached Fleur easily. 'I was expecting a shy little schoolgirl.'

'She's certainly not *that*!'

It was Julian who answered and Owen Lloyd who backed him up. 'What perfectly beautiful hair!'

'But such a worry, with that white skin!' Sheena pointed out in concerned tones. Her own skin gleamed with a year-round deep golden tan.

They were seated at the table and the meal began. Fleur had expected Matthew to join them as a matter of course, but it had been Matthew himself who had told her Sir Charles didn't care for children at the dinner table.

Of course he wouldn't! Fleur had thought, but Matthew was quite happy with the arrangement. It was much too late to wait for dinner in any case, and he dreaded being addressed by visitors in case his grandfather snorted at his immature replies. A brilliant man Sir Charles might be, but he wasn't a very tolerant one.

'You can begin serving, Maria,' he said to his unfailingly goodnatured Italian housekeeper. 'Wine, Julian, The wine. I don't remember seeing the wine.'

'The Pommerol '62,' said Julian, and didn't move. The light from the massive chandelier overhead played up his extravagant good looks. His hair was jet black, his skin polished bronze, and the eyes he turned towards his grandfather a startling sapphire. Though he always sounded smooth and respectful, it was apparent to everyone that he wasn't in the least intimidated by the imperious and short-tempered old man.

'All right, then.' Sir Charles gave a grunt of approval or disgust. Old as he was, he had even a more physically commanding presence than he had in his prime, and Fleur guessed Julian would be the same.

Dinner progressed, so superbly presented and so mouthwatering, Fleur's appetite picked up.

'Have you thought what you're going to do, Fleur?' Sheena asked.

'*Do?* Why, she's going to stay home, of course,' Sir Charles barked.

'Modern girls hate that,' said Sheena, and gave the old man a provocative smile.

'Excuse me, but I don't call what *you* do work!' Sir Charles retaliated with a marked lack of tact.

'Very lucrative, though,' Sheena continued to smile. 'I'm in P.R.,' she explained to Fleur, on the side. 'One of the big overseas fashion houses.'

'I'm sure they were very happy to get you.' Fleur's expressive eyes reflected her appreciation of the older girl's glossy appearance.

'Why, thank you.' Sheena looked surprised and a little flattered. She wasn't used to sincere compliments from her own sex and never paid them. 'What did you do yourself?'

'Office work. Particularly depressing.'

'It was my understanding you were to go on to university,' Sir Charles said a little stiffly.

'She can do that now,' Julian said evenly.

'That's not the point!'

'And what *is*?'

Fleur took a deep breath, intervening. 'I couldn't easily study when my mother required so much of my attention.'

'Of course!' Dr Alistair nodded his head at her like a kind and understanding wise old owl. 'What you need now is a period of calm and relaxation, the warm security of being with young Matthew.'

'Homecoming,' said Julian.

'Fair enough!' Sir Charles conceded. 'Now eat up your food. I have a couple of calls I must take tonight.'

Even to Fleur's uninformed palate the wine was very good, and as she bent to pick up her glass she was aware of Sheena's hard, speculative glance on her. There were many more of them until the men went off and the three women were left talking together.

'It can't be a comfortable situation for you, Fleur,' Sheena swung herself into an earnest conversation.

'In what way?' Charlotte was betrayed into asking the question, a lift to her strongly marked dark brows.

'Oh don't be so stuffy, Lottie.' Sheena reached over and touched the older woman's hand. 'A family like the Standfords can't keep all that many secrets.'

'Rifts happen everywhere,' Charlotte replied a little stiffly. 'Fleur was only a child when she was taken from Waverley. Short of kidnapping her, there was no way we could prevent it. My grandmother was frightfully upset by it all.'

'Yet Fleur isn't really family?' Sheena smiled at Fleur very gently.

'She was, and she is now!' Charlotte said flatly.

Sheena shrugged gracefully. 'You're all your mother, are you?' she asked. Her dark eyes appraised Fleur's vivid colouring.

'Her mother was a great beauty,' Charlotte said heavily.

'But surely Fleur is very pretty?' Sheena looked from one to the other in feigned bewilderment.

'My mother was dark. Dark hair, dark eyes,' Fleur explained. 'She was the most beautiful woman I've ever seen. I don't resemble her in the least.'

'That's true!' Charlotte's mouth had a tight, drawn look. 'Neither in looks nor personality. Matthew has nothing of his mother in him either.'

'You sound as though you're glad,' Sheena commented with uneasy challenge.

'I'm sure if you've heard all the stories,' said Charlotte, 'you'll know my sister-in-law hurt a lot of people.'

'Hurt and *was* hurt!' Anger flared in Fleur and she got swiftly to her feet. 'You'll excuse me, won't you? It's been rather an exhausting day.'

Vaguely she heard Charlotte call her name, but she was tired of all the wounding. Would it never cease? The night seemed the best place, the perfumed quiet of the garden. Without her inhibiting presence Charlotte would feel free to tell Sheena everything she wanted to know. As far as that went, Sheena probably knew more about the old tragedies than Fleur herself.

She slipped swiftly past the bronze statues in the hallway and out into the glorious tropical night. There were gardenias flowering somewhere and their perfume dominated a heady mixture of scents.

So many people who seemed to have hated her mother. What had she done? The old stories re-created themselves in Fleur's mind. As a young widow with a four-year-old daughter, her mother had met David Standford quite by accident. Ordinarily their lives would have never crossed but for a sudden rainstorm. They had been standing, unprotected, at a bus stop and David Standford had been moved to stop.

Who wouldn't, for an adorable four-year-old, he had often joked, but it was her mother's dangerous beauty that had captured him instantly and drove him to marry her despite a wealth of opposition. The Standfords had disliked Helena from the start, even Grandma Standford who had been so kind. For the one and only time in his life, David Standford disobeyed his grandfather, married his Helena and set in motion a series of conflicts that ended, inevitably, in tragedy.

Helena too had made a grave error in judgment. The Standford family, despite their great private fortune, had been visited often by tragedy. Charlotte, the eldest, David and Julian had lost their parents before Charlotte was in her teens. Their father, Richard, was killed in a mine disaster, having led men to safety in an extreme situation. Their mother, well advanced in her fourth pregnancy, had been so profoundly shocked she miscarried her child and died right under her doctor's stricken eyes. The baby lived on for two weeks, before it too abandoned the fight for life. After that, the children went to live with their grandparents, but only Julian thrived. Julian, the youngest, a man in his grandfather's mould, if you want.

Damn them, damn them all! Fleur muffled the

words in her throat. Her mother had been seduced by wealth and a high social position, and how dearly she paid for it. There were tears on her cheeks, but she didn't even know they were there.

'Fleur?'

Through the intensity of her thoughts she heard Julian's voice.

Instinct told her to run, to hide. The sky was encrusted with stars, but there was no moon tonight. Probably he had come to tell her she couldn't continue to act like an hysterical child. She ran lightly, like all creatures built for speed, but under the enveloping shadows of the trees a man's arm reached out and snaked around her waist.

'What is it? What's happened?'

His arm pulled her to him and suddenly she was leaning against him for support.

'Does it matter?' she asked emotionally. 'I only know the past will never be forgotten.'

'Then we must do as well as we can with what we've got,' he answered sombrely.

'*I'm* trying!' She tipped up her head to him, as though defying him to disagree.

'But you've always been a compassionate little creature. It's not in you to hate.'

'I don't think that's true!' Some fiery emotion was kindling inside her.

'You mean you hate *me*?'

With her deepest senses she knew she didn't, yet he menaced her. 'Let's not talk about it.' With an effort she broke away from him. 'My coming here has agitated Charlotte, hasn't it?'

'She wanted you to come, Fleur.'

'Yes, but for Matthew. She loves Matthew, I can see that.'

'He reminds her of David. David was her favourite brother.' He said it casually without the least bit of resentment.

'You mean Charlotte likes to be needed and you've never needed anybody.'

'And what do you really know of me, Fleur?' His hands came down on her bare shoulders, challenging her in every way there was. 'Do you think I would ever willingly injure you?'

'I had nothing to do with it,' she cried. 'It was my mother you ruined. Why were you so cruel, Julian, *tell* me?' She looked up into his dark face, but could only see the glitter of his eyes.

'We were all concerned for your mother,' he said a little harshly, 'but we couldn't help her. Helena was bent on self-destruction. She courted excitement and danger.'

'In what way? I've *got* to know the truth!'

'You more than anyone, Fleur, must have known the storms in her. She never spoke about her childhood, but it couldn't have been happy. Perhaps it even flawed her for life. She was always reaching for what she couldn't have.'

'You mean she wanted her own son!' Fleur choked on her own words.

'She *didn't*, Fleur.' He spoke with shattering conviction. 'From the moment Helena came into our home, she'd decided what she wanted.'

'The easy life, why not?' Fleur knew she was weeping again. 'She was never very strong, yet you begrudged her security, a home for her child.'

'You can't begin to know what it was like. Fleur. You were only a child.'

'And I wouldn't stay here another day, only for Matthew.'

'We're all doing it for Matthew,' he told her rather wearily. 'He hasn't got your spirit or self-reliance.'

'If you'll forgive my saying so, Sir Charles would crush anybody,' she said acidly.

'When we all know you don't give a damn about him and never have. I suppose you don't remember my grandmother used to get some of her best laughs watching you standing up to her husband. Ginger spunk, she used to call it, though you've always had hair like a flame.'

'I miss her,' Fleur murmured. 'Even now.' She was beginning to feel distinctly confused. Perhaps it was the wine. 'She was so gentle and kind. I never could understand how she came to marry Sir Charles.'

'I take it you've never fallen in love?' Gently he steered her back towards the house.

'I don't ever intend to.'

'Insofar as any of us *intend* to.' He laughed beneath his breath. 'Falling in love can happen very suddenly, in an instant.'

'You prefer to play games.'

'My goodness,' he said suavely, 'I'm amazed you've turned out so bitchy.'

'After all, I'm not a child any longer,' she pointed out.

'Certainly not.' They were coming back into the light and she saw the taunting smile on his face.

'Sheena?'

'Yes?'

'She's really stunning.'

'I think so.'

'Do you *ever* intend to marry anyone?' she asked curiously.

'I'm like you, darling,' he said jeeringly. 'I've seen too much unhappiness in my time.'

'Also you've inflicted quite a bit!'

'As a matter of fact, I've a remarkable record,' he pointed out dryly. 'All my women friends are still my friends.'

'Millionaires, particularly, are always popular.'

'I knew it wouldn't take you long to get over being nervous,' he drawled.

'No,' she said firmly, 'and I prefer it that way.'

'I always said redheads were the damnedest people.'

'Hi there, you two!' Sheena called, more stridently than she intended.

'How positively uncool!' Fleur observed maliciously. 'Doesn't Sheena know you see me in the light of a little cousin?'

'I never have done.'

'What's that supposed to mean?' she asked abruptly.

'You believe you're the only one who should be allowed to take a rise out of anyone?'

'Oh, *do* come up!' Sheena called more flutingly, and to make sure of it, descended the stairs. 'Lottie and I were so afraid we'd upset you, Fleur.'

'Obviously that wasn't your intention.'

'Of course not!' Sheena assured her, looking at the younger girl more closely. 'To tell you the truth, I'm longing for us to be friends.'

'That's very kind of you,' Fleur answered with a crooked little smile. Sheena had moved like a homing bird to Julian's side, her bare golden arm twined possessively around his own.

'Not at all!' Sheena was decisive, intent on conquering all the family. 'I'll ring you one day this week and we'll have lunch.'

It was the last thing Fleur wanted, but she nodded her head. Sheena seemed like an extremely determined person and a quick lunch might save a lot of trouble. She moved up the steps and into the entrance hall while Sheena's deliberately cultivated husky tones drifted clearly on the night air:

'Darling, you've been neglecting me!'

A silence. A breathy laugh, full of excitement.

You poor fool! Fleur thought, and walked away.

CHAPTER THREE

FLEUR slept late in the morning and when she finally opened her door Matthew was hovering outside.

'Gosh, I thought you were never going to wake up!' He smiled widely, full of peace and contentment.

'It's all the quiet. I'm used to the sounds of traffic.'

'You don't have to worry. You can do anything you like,' Matthew promised expansively.

'Good.' Fleur put her arm around him. 'Then I want you to come and sit beside me while I have my breakfast.'

'I would have waited,' Matthew sounded apologetic, 'only Lottie grabbed me by the arm and made me have some cereal. I don't understand what's so great about cereal!'

'I'll tell you, fibre in the diet,' Fleur answered playfully. 'You can't have too much fibre.'

'Except Grandfather won't touch it, and I believe he'll live until he's a hundred.'

'Some people are blessed with perfect health,' Fleur said soothingly. 'All in all Sir Charles takes very good care of himself.'

'Oh, by the way, Uncle Julian wants to speak to you,' Matthew told her.

'Hasn't he gone yet?' Fleur looked at her step-brother in surprise.

'He's been exchanging phone calls for the past hour,' Matthew told her. 'Business. It's going on all the time.' Clearly the idea terrified him.

'Where is he, in the study?'

'I'll come with you.' Matthew looked at her soberly. 'I hope I never have to take Uncle Julian's place. The demands are colossal. Even when he's sleeping, I'm sure his brain is ticking over.'

'Ah, yes,' Fleur said dryly, and resisted the temptation to say any more. Her own feelings about Julian were so complicated it was in her best interests to continue to regard him as her enemy.

The door to the study was open, and as they hesitated outside, looking in, Julian put his hand over the mouthpiece of the phone and called to her:

'Come in, Fleur. I won't be a moment.'

'What do you feel like for breakfast?' Matthew asked her. 'I'll tell Maria.'

'Don't try and give me cereal,' she smiled at him. 'I usually have orange juice, a boiled egg and coffee.'

'No toast?'

'I'll have it today,' she assured him.

'Beaut! I'll join you,' said Matthew with satis-faction, and turned away. 'Don't be long.'

Inside the study, Fleur let her eyes stray around the room. It had a remarkably satisfying look about it; three walls lined with bookshelves from floor to ceiling, a magnificent Persian rug over the

polished floor, a deeply comfortable sofa and arm-
chairs and behind the rich, dark mahogany desk, a
bay window that afforded a beautiful view over
the lake. Blue lotus lilies thrust their gorgeous
heads above the still, emerald surface and an enormous jacaranda trailed its lavender branches
almost to the water. It was quite a sight to greet
anyone's eyes, but Julian had his back to it, still
talking on the phone.

Fleur glanced at his downbent black head and
her heart thudded unpleasantly, a warning system
to remind her that though he delighted her eye and
beguiled her ear she knew his true character.

You arrogant devil! she murmured inwardly. He
exuded power, even sitting down with his face half
in shadow.

Unexpectedly he looked up, reading her transparent face, the green eyes brilliant and accusing.
'Ummm,' he murmured agreement on the phone
but continued to pin Fleur's gaze.

He was doing it deliberately, she knew that, but
she could no more look away from him than a doe
from a tiger. The very thought made her shiver
and at that moment his eyes released her. He
reeled off a few more incisive instructions to a key
employee, then hung up.

'Sit down, Fleur,' he said with calm authority.

She glanced at her watch as though she could
scarcely spare the time, but her knees were shaking
so much she was secretly grateful for the support
of an armchair.

'Did you sleep well?'

Was there derision in his sapphire eyes? 'Yes, thank you,' she answered coolly. 'What did you want to see me about?'

'You'll be needing money, credit cards, that kind of thing. Which means you'll have to take a trip into town. I can arrange most things, but the bank will be needing your signature.'

'I have very little until the house is sold up.' She couldn't help it, the words came out almost heatedly.

'You have the money my grandmother left in trust for you. I have the authority to release a considerable amount now.'

Fleur swallowed on a mounting lump in her throat. 'May I ask how much Grandma Standford left me?'

Quite casually Julian named a figure that made her gasp. 'But why would she do that?'

'It's not a great deal, Fleur, as money goes,' he told her unemotionally, 'but my grandmother always cared for you and worried about your future. She left you what she could as a form of security. Matthew is well provided for; you weren't.'

'I don't know whether I should take it.' She bent her head so he couldn't see the sudden glitter of tears in her eyes.

'Don't you remember Grandma Standford as a friend?' He got up and came round to her, resting back against the desk.

'I do.' My _only_ friend, it was on the tip of her tongue to say, but it wasn't necessary anyway because he lifted her chin and read it in her eyes.

'Do you want to come into town with me this morning?'

'Not today. I don't want to leave Matthew.' She took a deep breath and tilted her chin so he had to let it go.

'All right, then, tomorrow. You drive, of course?'

'You saw the car.' Or maybe he didn't, it was so small.

'Then you'll be wanting another one.' He walked back around the desk and began to clip a sheaf of papers into a file. 'Any preference?'

'Are you suggesting I can have a Rolls?'

'I don't think you would reach the wheel.' His mocking eyes flicked over her slight, petite figure.

'If you *must* know,' she said a little sharply, the colour in her cheeks, 'I'm a good driver, and I want to take Matthew to the beach. Often.'

'You say it as though I'm going to bodily prevent you.'

'Then you don't mind?'

'It's O.K. with me.' He smiled at her, looking for a moment so like her beloved stepbrother, her heart turned over. 'You always were a very trustworthy and responsible little thing. You could even try the pool,' he added. 'I had it converted to salt, but I never see a soul in it.'

'I think Aunt Charlotte was worried about all those recurring infections.'

'Well, darling,' he glanced at her very dryly, 'I have it on excellent medical authority that the risk of infection should be considerably reduced. I'd like to be able to spend more time with Matt, only I assure you I've very little freedom at all.'

'*You?*' she queried.

'Don't you know I work a twenty-four-hour day?'

'I'm sure you don't have to.' She stared up at him. 'There must be hundreds of people you can give orders to.'

'Unfortunately most people are frightened of giving orders, didn't you know?'

'I know you're not one of them.'

'Just as well,' he said cynically. 'What would happen to the Standford fortunes if I suddenly took off into the blue?'

'But you'd never want to.' The sarcasm was there in her voice and her shimmering eyes. 'You enjoy being rich and splendid.'

Julian laughed and tied up her gaze again. 'Do you really think I'm that?'

Such was feminine perversity she couldn't keep the unwilling attraction out of her eyes. 'I feel for Miss Lloyd,' she told him.

'She's quite old enough to look after herself. You aren't.'

'May I go now?' She simply couldn't stay there duelling with him.

'Sure,' he answered with mockery in his voice. 'I'll take you into town tomorrow. Plan on a full day. You'll be needing lots of things—plenty of clothes. Sheena might be able to help you there.'

'I can help myself, thank you very much!'

'I suppose I should expect a redhead to be naturally explosive,' he drawled. 'I only meant Sheena is a beautiful dresser and she knows all the best places to go.'

'I can *make* clothes,' Fleur said thriftily, proud of her ability both as a cutter and a sewer.

'Please, darling, don't!' he glanced at her, his eyes half closed with amused mockery. 'You'll be expected to be perfectly turned out for every occasion—the price of being a Standford.'

'Oh, but I'm not!' she threw back at him aggressively.

'But you're stuck with us.'

That was undeniable, and for an instant she bitterly resented it, until she remembered her stepbrother.

'Then you have no objection if Matthew and I go where we please?'

'Within reason, flower-face!' He lifted his briefcase on to the desk and put the blue file into it. 'Certainly not Europe or the States. Not just yet. If you're especially good, I'll take you both over to Japan when I go. Probably the end of March.'

'Won't we be in the way?' She knew perfectly well their Japanese business connections.

'It sounds crazy, I know, but I'd probably enjoy it. Once you get going I'm sure you have a fascinating tongue.'

He was ready to go now, walking towards her, and her heart gave that funny little leap again. 'Have a nice day,' he said.

'I think you ought to know I'm going to do

everything I can to preserve my independence.'
She gazed up at him defiantly, knowing too well
the authoritarian approach of the Standfords.

'Exactly my view of your character!' He put out
a hand and twined one of her silky curls around
his finger. 'It's wonderful to have you back, Fleur.'

So great was his destructive fascination she literally leapt away from him. 'You're wasting your
time trying to charm me!'

'Oh—is that what I'm trying to do?' He pulled
her to him with confidence and kissed the top of
her head, just like a baby. 'Now I've got to get
going. I have a lot of work to do. See you tonight.'

She scarcely seemed to taste her breakfast, her
thoughts coming back abruptly to how she felt
tucked up against his side. It wasn't reassuring to
know that though her mind was free from his
domination, her flesh was weak. Starved of deep
and demonstrative affection as she had been, it
was too easy for him to deal with her. She could
still feel his touch in her hair.

'What's the matter?' Matthew asked.

'Why, nothing!' Fleur turned her dreamy face
towards him. 'What are we going to do today?'

'Oh, anything you like. Sit around and talk, go
into town, go for a drive. *Can* you drive?' he asked
her.

'Of course I can!' She blinked at him in mock
affront. 'Uncle Julian is going to get me a car so
we can trip around the countryside.'

'Is he really?' Matthew looked greatly pleased.
'What kind?'

'I suppose a jolly old Daimler.'

Charlotte came back on to the sunlit terrace, overhearing the conversation. 'I hope, Fleur, you're a good driver?'

'I enjoy it,' Fleur made a valiant effort to answer pleasantly. The last thing she wanted to do was antagonise Charlotte even when she could see the older woman's attitude towards Matthew was very possessive. 'Naturally I'll be very careful while I'm finding my way around. I'm used to heavy traffic.'

'Adams is available quite often,' Charlotte pointed out, and sat down under the yellow and white striped umbrella.

Matthew looked appalled. 'Gosh, Lottie, who wants to travel around in a Rolls? It's all right for Granddad, but he's an old man.'

'Adams is an excellent driver,' said Charlotte, 'and we can't safeguard you enough.'

'We don't want to go with Adams,' Matthew said in an odd, flat voice. 'That's why Uncle Julian is getting Fleur the car.'

'Truly, Aunt Charlotte, it will be all right,' Fleur murmured, and folded her linen napkin.

'What kind of car is it?' Charlotte asked. 'It would be just like Julian to buy you something highly unsuitable.'

'I don't really know.' Fleur was a little upset at Charlotte's tone. 'I had a Datsun myself.'

'Then it's going to be an almighty jump to a Daimler.' Charlotte glanced sideways at Matthew's mutinous face.

'I was only joking.' Fleur had been prepared for Charlotte's opposition. 'I expect it will be another Datsun.'

'Not likely!' Matthew burst out laughing. 'Uncle Julian loves cars. He's not going to bring home the usual little runabout.'

'We'll see!' Fleur took a deep breath and tried to change the subject. 'I thought I'd get Matthew started on a swimming programme, Aunt Charlotte.'

'I wish you wouldn't, Fleur,' Charlotte said with chilly displease on her face. 'I realize you mean well, but pools have caused no end of trouble for Matthew. He's had ear infections, eye infections and infections on the chest. I'm tired of all the worry.'

'I can see that,' Fleur started, 'but Matthew hasn't really tried our own pool since Julian had it converted to salt.'

'That's true,' Matthew nodded, none too happily himself. 'I'm not really the sporting type, Fleur.'

'But you desperately need the exercise.' Fleur caught his hand and held it. 'Swimming is marvellous for asthmatics. I'm a good swimmer, but we could get a coach if you liked.'

'Please do not attempt to go over my head,' Charlotte put in rather grimly. 'Matthew is my responsibility and has been for a long time.'

'Please, Aunt Charlotte,' Fleur's green eyes were beseeching, 'we won't help him this way. It would be better to risk an infection and build up his chest. I'm sure it's only because of the Standford frame that he's not in a far worse condition.'

'Can't you just accept what I'm saying to you, Fleur?' Charlotte challenged.

'No, Aunt Charlotte, I can't!' Fleur answered gravely. 'I've come all this way for Matthew, no one else. With all due respect, and I know how deeply you care for him, I have a responsibility too. It's a well proven fact that swimming is wonderful therapy for anyone with Matthew's condition.'

'Do you think we haven't tried?' Charlotte asked sharply.

'His uncle thinks he ought to try.' She *had* to use Julian's authority as a last resort.

'Julian has never been known to sit up nights,' Charlotte remarked grimly. 'He's had perfect health—*perfect*. Right from a child.' Her voice flickered with an odd bitterness. 'It was David who suffered all the little ailments. Always David.'

Scarcely Julian's fault, Fleur thought incredulously. It was very obvious David had been Charlotte's favourite, but it was Matthew they were talking about now.

'In any case, there are ear-plugs that Matthew can wear while he's swimming,' she said as pleasantly as she could. 'I'm sure he's having tons of vitamin C.'

'Actually I'm not!' Matthew cast a quick glance at his aunt. 'I have an orange drink every day, but Lottie took me off that white stuff.'

'The case for massive doses of any vitamin has not been proven to my mind,' Charlotte said formidably, as though she expected an argument.

'Couldn't we ask Dr Alistair?' Fleur suggested, stifling her irritation. 'It seems to me Matthew has a special need of it in much larger doses than orange juice.'

'I don't doubt you'll ask Hugh,' Charlotte sighed. 'Looking back, as a child, you had a flair for offering your opinion.'

'Does it annoy you, Aunt Charlotte?' Fleur tried not to get angry, but she was all the same.

'You're a very positive person, Fleur,' Charlotte said finally. 'It's natural you want to rush in and help, but you must defer to my judgment. I really do know what's best for Matthew and I fear all we can do is wait for him to grow out of it.'

Short of launching into a full scale argument, there was little else Fleur could say. Crushing down her natural thoughts of rebellion, she began to speak about the beauty of the grounds.

Charlotte, a keen gardener, nodded agreeably. 'In the spring, of course, we have the most wonderful display of azaleas and camellias. It's a place of enchantment then.'

'I remember,' Fleur answered pleasantly, trying not to feel hurt and rebuffed. She had been twelve years old when she left.

'Of course she does!' Matthew burst out in an irked voice. 'She remembers everything!'

'Except what drove us all apart.' Abruptly Charlotte stood up, her mind apparently far back in the past. 'Excuse me, won't you, children, I have things to attend to.'

'Certainly.' Fleur made a little bobbing gesture out of her chair.

'End of conversation,' Matthew hissed as they both watched Charlotte's tall, straight-back figure disappear through the French doors. 'Don't take any notice of Lottie,' he begged his stepsister. 'She's a good person really, but she's got lots of hang-ups.'

'You can say that again!' Fleur gave a tense little laugh. 'I suppose it's not easy being the unmarried daughter of the house.'

'Actually she's quite keen on the gardener,' Matthew volunteered in a hushed, confidential tone.

'*What?*' Fleur could feel her mouth fall open.

'Not an ordinary gardener,' Matthew amended, 'he's in landscape construction and design. Uncle Julian thinks he's brilliant. He put the pool in and the surrounds, then Uncle Julian got him to do the lily pond.'

'More like a lake!' Fleur glanced around at the shimmering sheet of water. 'He *is* clever—very creative. What's his name?'

'Kurt Werner. He and Lottie have long, earnest conversations about soils and chemicals and wonderful things like that. I used to think Uncle Julian was encouraging them because then he got pergolas done and the terraced gardens and, of course, the grounds need looking after they're so big. Kurt's men attend to that and we usually see him once or twice a week.'

'Do you like him?' Fleur asked, unable to picture Charlotte in a tender moment.

'Oh yes,' Matthew's answer was boyishly off-hand. 'He's all right, but he's very quiet. Grandfather doesn't like him at all. He calls him Attila and poor old Lottie hates it. I think that's why Grandfather keeps it up. He can be quite cruel sometimes. I know, because I overhead Uncle Julian telling him.'

'Well, well!' Fleur stared into Matthew's blue eyes. 'That's a surprising twist. I'm looking forward to meeting Kurt.'

'Then you probably will this afternoon,' Matthew grinned. 'Try and get him to talk.'

Mindful of Charlotte's opposition, Fleur didn't venture into the pool, nor did she suggest it to Matthew; a hardship, because it was very hot and the brilliantly glistening water looked wonderfully inviting. Lunch passed uneventfully and afterwards brother and sister went for a long stroll around the neighbourhood admiring all the architect-designed homes and the well kept gardens ablaze with colour. Matthew was in his element pointing out different designs and the ones he favoured, and Fleur looked at him with deep affection.

'One day you'll be designing a special home for yourself.'

'We'll share it,' Matthew assured her.

'I take the view you'll be married by then,' Fleur smiled at him. 'Wives don't take kindly to sharing their husbands.'

'Who'd want a husband who was wheezing all

the time?' Matthew stopped suddenly and turned around to face her. 'You haven't seen me when I'm having an attack.'

Fleur answered positively, 'You can beat this thing, Matthew. How about trying?'

'But *how*?'

'By telling yourself every day you're going to get better. As well we're going to add practical help to the psychology.'

'Thanks very much.' Matthew's smile widened bit by bit and he started walking again. 'Does this mean I have to do physical jerks? Uncle Julian has already bought me dumbbells and things.'

'Come on now,' Fleur slipped her hand into his, 'exercise isn't all that bad. Wouldn't you like to get better?'

'I sure would!'

'Right then, let's astonish the experts!'

By the time they got home, it was mid-afternoon and just as Matthew had said they found Charlotte in her wildflower garden talking to a blond giant of a man with shy blue eyes and a fine, fair skin that was freckled and reddened by the harshness of a tropical sun.

Charlotte, with a curious flush in her cheeks, made the introductions and Fleur found her hand taken and enveloped by what she could only think of as a gentle paw.

'I'm so pleased to meet you, Mr Werner,' she offered smilingly. 'I've been admiring all the changes you've made.'

'I'm so glad.' The voice was slow and deep and

heavily accented. 'But the ideas all came from Mr Standford in the first place.'

'Nevertheless you brought them to life.'

Charlotte looked pleased. 'Kurt is an artist, you see.'

It was as plain as it could have been that Charlotte was very kindly disposed towards their landscape gardener, and Fleur felt her heart soften. 'I thought I'd have a cup of coffee,' she said. 'Anyone like one?'

Kurt Werner looked startled and even blushed and Charlotte, too, lost her stern composure. 'I'd prefer tea, thank you, Fleur. You'll join us, won't you, Kurt?'

'I would be most happy to.' The uneasiness vanished out of Kurt's faded blue eyes. 'Tea for me, thank you, Miss Fleur.'

'I'll bring it out on the rear terrace,' Fleur smiled. 'Matthew, come and help me.'

They found Maria in the kitchen busy making a rich, luscious torte that Sir Charles particularly liked with his after-dinner coffee.

'Oh, that looks scrumptious,' said Fleur, and came to stand beside Maria's ample figure. 'Would you mind, Maria, if I make tea and coffee?'

'Allow me,' smiled Maria, and began to wipe her hands.

'No, please.' Fleur touched her shoulder. 'Go on with what you're doing. I'm not used to being waited on.'

'Is no bother.' Maria looked uncertain.

'Fleur's making tea for Charlotte and *Mr*

Werner,' Matthew told the housekeeper round-eyed.

To Fleur's astonishment Maria broke into Italian.

'What does *that* mean?' Fleur looked at her stepbrother for enlightenment.

'It means Maria is surprised.'

Maria did indeed look surprised, but as Fleur filled the electric kettle and plugged it in, Maria walked away to the pantry and returned with a couple of cake tins.

'Matthew,' she ordered, ' 'elp your sister. You know where the cups and saucers are.'

In the end, it turned out to be a very pleasant little tea-party. They spoke exclusively about plants and gardens and when Kurt went off, Charlotte accompanied him ostensibly to confirm an order for hundreds of new seedlings.

'What did I tell you?' grinned Matthew. 'She's sweet on him, poor old Lottie.'

'And what's wrong with that?' Fleur gave him a close stare. 'He's a very nice man.'

'The trouble is,' said Matthew, ignoring her, 'Lottie can't make a friend of him.'

'Why not?' Fleur loaded the tray.

'Grandfather would never hear of it.'

'The old snob!'

'He is and he isn't,' Matthew said. 'Just cynical mostly, I suppose. He probably thinks Kurt is after Lottie's money.'

'He's not that sort of person.'

'Lucky for him,' Matthew shrugged, and

polished off the last piece of cake. 'Lottie had a disastrous romance a couple of years ago. *He* was definitely after her money. Uncle Julian found out and told her so. You can bet your life he's had Kurt checked out as well, so I really think Kurt must like Lottie for herself.'

'Good grief, it's enough to give a girl ulcers,' Fleur remarked soberly. 'I'm glad I'm not an heiress.'

'I'll tell you something,' Matthew grinned, and took the tray off her, 'you're the first person who's ever offered Kurt tea on the terrace!'

CHAPTER FOUR

WHETHER she wanted Sheena's company or not, Fleur found that she had it.

'You're tired, aren't you, you poor darling?'

'Just a little.' Fleur stood in a green silk chiffon evening dress the colour of her eyes. It was the day of her shopping trip and Sheena had accompanied her. And what a treasure she was! She knew everyone who was anyone in the fashion world and her taste was superb.

'What about something of Zandra Rhodes?' Sheena said to the fantastic-looking woman who owned the exclusive boutique. 'Fleur has such vivid colouring she could take it.'

'I have just the thing!' the woman gushed, filled with bliss at having sold more clothes in one morning than she had done in the past month. Besides, the girl could carry any dress she had, she was so slight and pretty and chic, and Sheena Lloyd was one of her best customers.

To Fleur's surprise, Sheena was looking genuinely pleased and excited. Sheena loved clothes as a couturier loves them and it gave her intense satisfaction to be able to assist Julian's young relative in her choice of a complete wardrobe.

The Zandra Rhodes looked brilliant, the quilted gold satin bandeau fitting snugly over Fleur's small, high bosom.

'Now let's see,' Sheena put her glossy head to one side, 'is there anything you haven't got?'

'A raincoat?'

'Naughty!' Sheena gave her confident laugh. 'No one owns a raincoat in Queensland. Well, we might as well take a break and have lunch. Afterwards we'll get your hair shaped. It's very pretty, but I know just the man who can cut into the curl.'

They went to the best restaurant in town, and if Fleur expected a little casual conversation she soon found Sheena was subjecting her in point of fact to the third degree.

'Now I insist you tell me what you've been doing all these years. *All* of it. I do so want to understand.'

Why can't you understand it's none of your business? Fleur thought, but offered crumbs of information. Sheena gobbled it up very greedily, but only toyed with her food. Slim as she was, she had a weight problem and though she dined out very frequently she seldom swallowed more than a couple of mouthfuls of, most often, grilled fish.

'Of course you're going to have a problem with Charlotte.' Sheena sipped at her white wine. 'She's over-protective of Matthew.'

'I suppose it would get you that way,' Fleur answered a trifle briskly.

'She's not young either.' Sheena dug a fork fiercely into the salad. 'I do so feel sorry for her. No life of her own. Not that she's an easy person. We get on quite well, though I do have to make the effort. All for Julian, of course.' Sheena looked up and smiled into Fleur's eyes. 'I could do absolutely anything for Julian, except forget him.'

'He's all yours.' Fleur spoke before she knew it, then felt dismayed.

'What's *that* supposed to mean?' Sheena countered, narrow-eyed.

'High-powered men might be very glamorous, but I wouldn't care to be the woman who tried to match them.'

'Maybe not,' Sheena released her breath, 'but I've been searching for Julian all my life. He's the one man I've met who has everything!'

Except a heart. Fleur smiled and nodded to the waiter to take her plate away.

While they were waiting for coffee, Sheena didn't spare her. Julian was so utterly special, so alive and fascinating, so dedicated to big business at which he was brilliant. He was almost completely in control now that Sir Charles had turned eighty and according to Sheena he enjoyed a tremendous popularity with the miners, something his legendary grandfather had never achieved. Though she never said it, Sheena undeniably hinted, he was also brilliant in bed.

Fleur cared nothing for their sexual adventures. Of course he'd be brilliant; one had only to look at him to see that.

Almost two hours passed at the hairdresser's (Sheena had her hair done as well), but when Fleur finally looked at herself she had to admit Sheena's hairdresser had a magical way with the scissors. He had taken her short cap of curls and somehow set all the curl free as he tamed it. It clustered around her small head, defining the beautiful shape of the skull with little fiery splashes of curl drawn gently on to her white forehead. It wasn't a fringe at all, yet it made the most of her eyes. They looked very green and enormous.

'Beautiful!' the hairdresser brought his head down to Fleur's level and smiled into her mirrored eyes. 'Next time it will be even better!'

'Julian will be pleased!' Sheena stood up and tossed her gleaming mane back. 'Now you look just right to be a Standford.'

The remark put Fleur into a slow burn and she was still smarting at the end of the afternoon when Julian picked her up. Today it was a Daimler Double Six, but it could just as well have been the silver Maserati or the Porsche 924 in the garage.

And that's what money's for! Fleur thought wryly, and slipped quickly into the bucket seat.

'Well, how did it go?' Julian's blue eyes just barely flickered over her, yet she drew in her breath sharply.

'Sheena was a great help,' she said demurely.

'No other comment?'

'It's a nice little car.'

'Less cumbersome than the Rolls,' he answered in the same, dry tone. 'I like your hair.'

'Sheena again. She knows everyone.'

'You look utterly, totally, the most expensive

baby in the world,' he told her.

'Thank you. I did spend a lot of money.'

'What's wrong with that?'

'Nothing. It's too good to be true.' She looked out the window at the passing traffic. 'Why is it there are no animals at Waverley?'

'As in pets?' he answered a little sarcastically.

'Exactly.' He never did anything for the sweetness of her temper.

'Animal hair, darling, since you ask.'

'*Oh*.' However much she disliked the way he answered her, she had to accept it. 'I didn't think. Is Matthew supposed to be allergic to it, then?'

'God knows!' Julian said soberly. 'We've covered just about everything.'

'I think he'd love a dog,' said Fleur. 'A couple of them, with all that wonderful space to roam around in.'

'I understand flower gardens are very popular with puppies.'

'We could get full grown dogs from the pound. Think what it would mean to them to be given a good home.'

'I'm certain Charlotte will have something to say to that.' Smoothly he overtook a slow moving vehicle.

'We all know you're the boss, Julian.' She stole a brief glance at his handsome, chiselled profile. 'Just a prick of a needle would tell us if Matthew really is allergic. Somehow I don't think he is. We patted plenty of dogs when we were out walking yesterday with no kind of unfavourable reaction. I think it would be a lovely surprise to present him with a couple of pets.'

'It would be a surprise, certainly.' His mouth quirked in a smile. 'You must let me discuss it with Charlotte first.'

'And please, Julian, while you're at it,' Fleur turned to him earnestly, 'mention about the pool.'

'I've a feeling you already have.'

'And Aunt Charlotte doesn't approve. I understand how she feels, but I've promised Matthew we'd start on a swimming programme.'

'Congratulations if you've got him interested. Matt is a lot like David. My brother never was interested in sports.'

'While you excelled at everything.'

'Yes, ma'am. Don't expect me to apologise for it.' His resonant voice had gone slightly hard.

'Did you ever?'

'A lot when I was a boy. David was the elder. It was for him to shine.'

'Are you trying to tell me he was jealous?' The way he said it made it all believable.

'Not really.' Julian frowned and his winged black brows drew together. 'David had a different temperament altogether, He wasn't at all competitive, but Grandfather in particular gave him a bad time. He thought if he pushed David more, it would turn him into an achiever, but David didn't react that way at all.'

'No.' After a minute Fleur said a little more. 'I've tried hard to remember Uncle David, but my recollections are so hazy.'

'You were only a little girl after all.' He half turned his head towards her, but he didn't smile.

'I remembered *you* very well.' Without thinking it came out, the bitterness unmistakable in her pretty voice. Memories came flooding back; the way she used to run after him, reluctant to let him out of her sight. There was an excitement about Julian, a radiance, that made lesser mortals want to bask in it.

'Now you're in worse danger,' he said oddly, and his sapphire eyes flashed over her expressive face.

'How?' She hated the fact that her voice shook.

'All you get is the warning.' Unexpectedly he laughed. 'Poor little Fleur! Your eyes tell me an enormous amount of things.'

'Then I'll take care not to look at you!'

'I'm sorry I can't do the same for you, but you've done everything under the sun to attract and dazzle.'

'Never *you*,' she whispered, in shock.

'Oh?' he gave her a crooked smile. 'We're not related. You told me yourself how pleased you were about it.'

'And every time you look at me, you must remember why.' Fleur tried desperately to quiet her agitated heart.

'Every time I look at you, I see *only* you.' The gravity of Julian's voice matched his expression. 'The innocent little pawn in a tragic game.'

'You're telling me something, Julian,' she said angrily, what is it?'

'I don't think you could handle it.'

'Why don't you try me?'

'No.' His beautiful blue eyes touched her briefly and every nerve in her body quickened. 'Have you ever been in love, Fleur?'

'I don't trust any man,' she said decisively.

'You trusted me once.'

'And you were the one to show me what a fool I was!'

'A very sweet little fool.'

She was startled and shocked by the tenderness in his voice.

'Please can't we talk about Matthew?' she begged.

'Don't panic.' He lowered his speed as they turned on to the narrow road that led to the Standford estate. 'I'll speak to Charlotte tonight.'

Charlotte, as Fleur anticipated, was upset and disturbed that Fleur had her brother's backing.

'Believe me, nothing good will come of this,' Charlotte announced angrily, suddenly jolting the preoccupied Sir Charles into a curt spate of words.

'For God's sake, Charlotte,' he didn't bother to hide his annoyance, 'give this thing a go. Your own methods have achieved nothing in all these years. The boy's been practically an invalid.'

'Very well.' Stopped short, Charlotte had to catch back her rising temper. 'If you really think I need advice from a mere child!'

'Why not?' Sir Charles stood up and gave his granddaughter a sharp smile. 'There's nothing wrong with it so far as I can see.' He caught up a file he was looking at and turned on his heel. 'Come on, Julian, I want some advice on that Jock McLean. His background is too political.'

After the men had left, Charlotte sat on in an aggressive silence.

'Please don't be angry with me, Aunt Charlotte,' said Fleur with all her natural sweetness.

'You mean well, Fleur,' Charlotte burst out, 'but you simply don't *know*. Haven't I got enough on my hands without having Matthew sick again?'

'I'm here now to help you.'

'Forgive me if I don't see it that way.' Quickly Charlotte stood up. 'When you *see* Matthew having an attack, you'll understand.'

And perhaps I will. Left on her own, Fleur went to the piano and sat down. She was beset now by worry, anxious about Matthew's wellbeing, but she had to try. Matthew *did* need building up. She couldn't sit back and accept Charlotte's opinion, yet overriding Charlotte made her feel guilty.

The feeling of her fingers on the smooth keys reassured her. Her troubled thoughts switched from the tensions within the house to the calm beauty of a Chopin nocturne. She began softly, then because she was accomplished the piano gathered volume. The safest thing to do wasn't always the best.

Considering Charlotte's anxiety and gloomy predictions Matthew and Fleur spent a full week in and out of the pool with Matthew remaining blessedly free of any kind of complication. Matthew, in fact, to his own astonishment was thoroughly enjoying himself.

'I think if I really trained, I could be darned good,' he told Fleur after she had let him beat her.

'That's the way!' She reached out to ruffle his crisply glittering curls. 'I'll speak to Julian tonight about a coach.'

'Oh no, a coach would scare me stiff.' Matthew's pleasure seemed to ebb.

'All right, whenever you say,' Fleur answered casually. 'Let's try another lap.'

Inside the house, Charlotte heard their laughter and shrieks and her anxieties began to fade a little. Matthew was responding to his sister's love and attention like her plants to water. Kurt was coming tomorrow. What a splendid idea of Fleur's to invite him to have tea with them. Picking up her exquisite needlework, Charlotte walked outside to the pool area and found herself a comfortable chair out of the sun's glare.

'Watch me, Lottie!' Matthew called, and Charlotte put up her free hand and waved. It was incredible how much better her beloved nephew was looking, tanned and healthy from this distance, though much too thin. If she narrowed her eyes he could easily pass for David at the same age. And thinking of David, Charlotte avoided looking in Fleur's direction. She hadn't the heart for it. Yet.

The following afternoon Julian drove Fleur's new car home.

'For goodness' sake——' Charlotte burst out.

'Isn't it *beaut*!' Used to expensive big cars, Matthew was thrilled with the small red Alfetta. He raced down the driveway, pulling Fleur along with him.

Julian, all six feet two of him, was withdrawing from the small car. He had taken off his jacket and loosened his tie and his blazing sexuality never seemed more pronounced.

'It's for Fleur, isn't it?' Matthew called happily.

'For you both, but Fleur has to do the driving.'

'Gee, you're good to us,' grinned Matthew, and began opening the doors.

'Thank you, Julian.' Fleur came to stand at Julian's side.

'Is that all?'

'I wouldn't know what else you want.' She looked up at him quickly, titian head tilted, green eyes large and wondering.

He didn't answer, but just looked down at her, and she found to her dismay that she was trembling.

'Aren't you going to get in?' Matthew was demanding, surprised they hadn't heard him the first time.

'Well, don't just stand there, baby,' Julian said to her, 'take us for a drive.'

So for the next twenty minutes Fleur took them all for a ride. She was in an agony of nerves for the first minute or so, more from Julian's effect on her than any nervousness about driving the car, but Matthew's buoyant mood made them both relax.

'We'd better head home now,' Julian said smoothly. 'I'm having dinner out tonight.'

'Not *Sheena*!' Matthew threw back at him.

'Don't you like her?'

'She's all right,' Matthew waved a hand vaguely. 'Why don't you take Fleur out some time?'

'There's really nothing I'd like more!' Julian's voice was suave and mocking.

'I wouldn't go,' said Fleur.

'Did you hear that, Matt?'

'I think she wants to really.'

And suddenly in her mind Fleur saw Sheena in Julian's arms.

'Careful!' Matthew yelled at her, and looked backwards as though expecting to see a policeman on a motorcycle.

'Sorry.' Fleur eased her foot on the accelerator while Julian sat beside her quietly laughing.

One of the many things about him that terrified her, he seemed to be able to read her mind.

By the end of the following week Sir Charles decided Fleur had better meet a few people.

'Arrange something, Charlotte,' he told his granddaughter before he stomped out to the waiting Rolls. 'She's a captivating child and this is her home.'

'I suppose a party would be nice.' It was plain from Charlotte's sudden blush that she would have loved to include Kurt Werner in the guest list, though she knew perfectly well her grandfather would never accept him.

'Why don't you ask Kurt?' Fleur asked gently, reading Charlotte's face.

'Oh, heavens, no!' Charlotte put a watch on her unguarded face. 'He's a very shy person, as you know. He would only be uncomfortable.'

'I think he's more quiet than shy,' Fleur pointed out. 'Now that I've got to know him better I can see he's really a collected kind of person.'

'It wouldn't do, Fleur,' Charlotte sighed, but her eyes looked confused. 'My grandfather can be very unpleasant when the mood takes him. Whatever you and I may think of Kurt, he's just the gardener to Grandfather.'

'It seems to me you're entitled to make your own friends.' Fleur leaned against the windowsill and looked out over the magnificent rose garden.

'The ordinary things don't apply to me,' Charlotte told her brusquely. 'I've been kept down all my life.'

'It's for you, then, to break out.' Fleur turned round to survey Charlotte's tall, upright figure. 'You quite like Kurt, don't you?'

'I don't know.' Charlotte looked rattled. 'I don't know what he thinks of me.'

'I think he very much admires you,' Fleur answered truthfully, 'but he thinks a sensible man would know nothing can come of it. Your money terrifies him.'

'Why not?' Charlotte said bitterly. 'Everyone knows we've got too much.'

'Such a problem!' Fleur laughed.

'It can't safeguard any of us against loss and

grief.' Charlotte's stern face looked pained. 'All
we've ever had is money. When I was younger I
yearned for a man of my own to love, but I have
no capacity to attract.'

'That's not true, Aunt Charlotte!' Fleur responded to that bitter self-condemnation.

'You're a nice child,' Charlotte murmured unexpectedly. 'I thought when David brought your
mother to the house I'd never seen anyone more
beautiful in my life. I remember the way David
looked at her—Grandfather, every man that came
her way. Only Julian was immune. Your mother
broke up my engagement, did you know that?'

'No!' Fleur drew a sharp, amazed breath.

'It doesn't matter now. He wasn't worth anything.'

'She couldn't have done it deliberately.' Fleur
walked across the room to look into the older
woman's eyes.

'She did, Fleur,' Charlotte said tiredly. 'She was
like that, and then it was very easy for a woman
with her beauty. I think the reason she. . . .' Charlotte paused abruptly and broke off. 'A strange
moment to speak about the past. The only thing
any of us can do is forget it.'

But who was going to take away the pain? Fleur
stood for a long time looking out at the fragrant
bobbing heads of the roses.

The next morning she was awakened by Matthew
standing by her bedside. She sat up instantly alert,
staring at his white face.

'What is it, darling? Are you sick?'

Matthew nodded, seemingly unable to speak.

Fighting to control herself, Fleur reached for her robe and pulled it on. What had she done with her sweeping new ideas? Because of her, Matthew would suffer. Yet no terrible wheeze assailed her ears.

She got her arms around him, intending to take him back to his room, but instantly he went rigid and choked out a little cry.

'I'm going to be sick!'

The urgency in his voice galvanised her into action. She rushed him into the bathroom and stood there holding his head while he was violently ill. Afterwards he stood there shivering and she wiped his sick, clammy face with a flannel.

'Come back to bed, darling. We'll have to ring the doctor.'

He didn't seem capable of getting back to his own room, so Fleur folded back the top sheet and the blanket and helped him into her own bed. 'Will you be all right for a minute?' she bent over him anxiously. 'I must get help.'

'I had the most atrocious night,' he whispered. 'All terrible nightmares.'

'You're all right now. You're with me,' she said.

'I won't be sick again for a while,' Matthew tried to reassure her. 'There can't be anything left in my stomach.'

'I'll be as quick as I can.' Fleur patted him on the shoulder.

She charged down the hallway, totally disregarding the fact that she was still in her flimsy night attire. It was still early, she knew that by the quality of light, but there was sure to be someone about. She would check downstairs first, before knocking on Charlotte's door. Charlotte was an early riser and she always supervised the men's breakfasts.

As she flew down the staircase, Julian's voice came as a shock to her.

'What *is* it, Fleur?'

He stood in the entrance hall, staring up at her, and she hurled herself towards him.

'It's Matty. He's ill!'

'Damn!' Julian said no more but hurried them both back up the stairs.

Matthew was still lying in a crumpled heap on Fleur's bed and Julian went to him, placing a hand on the boy's brow.

'A bit of a temperature, not much. No sign of a wheeze.'

'Thank God!' Fleur had her hands joined at her breast like a little saint.

'Best be on the safe side and call the doctor,' Julian was still searching his nephew's face. 'What's the main trouble, Matt?'

'Something I ate,' said Matthew. 'I've been sick.'

'Ghastly, isn't it?' Julian smiled at him and smoothed back his hair. 'They've got injections these days to take care of nausea. I'll give the clinic a ring.'

'Too early,' Fleur told him, her small face desperate with worry. 'What *is* the time, Julian?'

He glanced at his watch, already dressed except for his jacket. 'Two minutes past seven. The call will be recorded and the doctor will be along as soon as he can.'

'Oh, I hope so.' She sat down on the chair beside the bed. 'How do you feel now, Matty?'

'A bit better.' Matthew tried, but his face looked a misery.

'I'll ring now.' Julian spoke with his usual calm authority. 'Fleur, stop worrying. It could very well be something he ate.'

Fleur's young face didn't look convinced. It was obvious she was punishing herself, and Julian caught her by the shoulder, saying briskly, 'You'd better get dressed.'

His blue eyes travelled over her, extraordinary eyes that alternately melted and stiffened her bones. A brief moment when she flushed deeply, then she leapt to her feet. 'Just give me a moment.'

In the bathroom she pulled on a T-shirt and cotton slacks and trod into her sandals. She didn't even glance in the mirror, all her thoughts with her stepbrother.

'Right?' Julian nodded to her briefly when she emerged again. 'I'll make that phone call.'

He had only been gone a moment when Matthew was sick again. Fleur held him, murmuring words of sympathy, and when they staggered back into the bedroom there was Charlotte in the doorway, her eyes full of dismay and hostility.

'Nobody ever takes any notice of me,' she said shortly. 'I told you, Fleur, all this swimming was a mistake.'

'I'm sorry, but we're not sure.' Fleur's expressive face pleaded with her not to start now.

'*Nonsense!*' snapped Charlotte, and charged into the room. 'Matthew dear, can you make your way back to your own room?'

'It's all right, I'll take him.' Julian had come back again, so darkly, vividly strong and handsome, Matthew looked paler and frailer than ever.

Julian lifted him like a featherweight and Charlotte and Fleur trooped along the corridor in his wake.

'What a shame when he was doing so well!' Charlotte said reproachfully.

'Stop fussing!' Julian put the boy down and turned on his sister with a speaking glance.

'Fleur,' said Matthew, 'don't go away.'

'Exactly,' Charlotte cried. 'I've looked after Matthew for years, now it's quite clear which one he wants!'

'*Charlotte,*' Julian warned in a smooth, cool voice, but Charlotte didn't want to be smoothed.

'You've always been Fleur's champion,' she said jerkily.

'Please, Aunt Charlotte, don't get excited!' Fleur could feel Matthew's thin hand begin to shake. Such tension and conflict was bad for him.

'Don't give me orders in my own home!' Charlotte's formidable face flushed.

'Stop it, Charlotte,' ordered Julian, putting his hand on her shoulder. 'The only thing that concerns us now is that Matthew is ill.'

'Then I'll leave *you* to look after him,' Charlotte announced with tears in her eyes. 'You and Fleur together, seeing you've got such faith in her.'

'You're becoming emotional, Lottie,' Julian told her. 'It's not like you.'

'I've got them, you know,' Charlotte countered, then turned abruptly on her heel.

'What's wrong with Lottie?' Matthew wheezed from the bed.

'Oh, *God*!' Fleur jumped up in anguish, her face pale and upset. 'You just stop that, you hear me?'

Matthew just lay there staring up at her.

'You're *not* going to have an attack,' she said with perfect surety. 'You're *not*. I won't let you. All you've got is a sick stomach.'

'A sick stomach? Is that all?'

'Yes,' said Fleur. 'So just be sensible. The doctor will be here shortly.'

Julian sat down on the side of the bed and took Matthew's flickering hand. 'A lot rests with you, Matthew. It's time you took yourself in hand. I want you to lie quietly and find your own centre, the place where you think your inner being resides.'

'Here?' Matthew pressed the area almost directly over his heart.

Julian nodded, still holding the boy's other hand. 'Now tell yourself what Fleur has said. You're *not* going to have an attack. You're *not*. You're *not*!'

Matthew closed his eyes and his thin body lay still. 'I'm not going to have an attack. I'm not. I'm *not*!' The lines of sickness and bewilderment began to smooth out of his face. He didn't look thirteen at all, but six, and Fleur was devastated by an upsurge of remembered grief.

With Julian and Matthew softly chanting she rushed out of the room and sought the privacy of the sitting room opposite.

Julian found her there a few minutes later, her face in her hands and her slender body shaking.

'You *mind* so much, Fleur.' He turned her into his arms.

'What if I'm to blame?' Responsibility flooded her. 'How can I tell him to just stop, when he can't? Who am I to tell anyone anything? I've hurt Charlotte, and it's the last thing I wanted.'

He went on holding her, easing her like a child. 'The wheeze has gone.'

'What?' She lifted her drowning eyes. 'Where did it go?'

'Evidently Matthew can banish it if he tries hard enough.'

'I'm hurting, Julian,' she told him, leaning against him with a sigh. Her head barely reached the top of his shoulder and his arm linked her closely to him at the waist.

'Fleur?' he queried, but she didn't answer.

He wasn't comforting her any more. Something had flashed between them. Something powerful. Always hidden from sight.

His hand speared through her short curls and he lifted her head to him.

'*Don't*, Julian,' she whispered, and it sounded like a prayer.

'I don't believe you.'

'Don't wreck my life!'

'You little fool,' he said curtly, but he didn't release her immediately.

The whole room seemed to be closing in on them, not a forbidding darkness, but a flame. There seemed no escaping him, then they heard Matthew's call.

'Fleur?'

'It's all right, I'm here!' She glanced quickly up at Julian, frightened of their intimacy.

'Go to him.' His blue eyes were remote. 'I'll wait until the doctor arrives.'

Less than an hour later the doctor was admitted to the sickroom. Fleur stood up as soon as she heard footsteps and went to the door. To her surprise, Julian had accompanied the doctor, a young man, and he quickly introduced them.

Anxious as she was, Fleur quite missed the bedazzled look that showed in the young doctor's eyes, to be almost reluctantly replaced by professionalism. Julian, as usual, missed nothing, and he directed the younger man's attention to the bed.

'How are you now, Matt?' he asked pointedly.

'A little better, I think.'

'Well, let's have a look at you,' Jon Talbot said cheerfully, surprised by the heavy thud of his own heart.

Fleur, still distressed, moved around to the other side of the bed and Julian went to stand by the window.

The examination continued, the young doctor

offering in an undertone the warming information he had read up Matthew's card. It was Dr McNulty, Matthew's usual doctor's day off, and the receptionist had called him at home.

'He was wheezing a little this morning.' Fleur's green eyes met the doctor's, barely even registering his fair good looks.

'Well, he's quite all right now.' Strong fingers beat a tattoo on Matthew's brown chest.

'I talked myself out of it.' Matthew reached for his sister's hand and held it.

'Good man!' The doctor opened his bag with a flourish. 'There's been a twenty-four-hour virus doing the rounds. A lot of my young patients have got it. I'll give you an injection to settle the tummy and you can spend the rest of the day in bed.'

Relief brought out Fleur's enchantingly sweet smile. 'We were so worried!'

'It's boring to be sick, isn't it, old man?' Dr Talbot looked at Matthew, then plunged the needle home. 'Nothing to eat, just sips of water. He'll be back to normal by tomorrow. If I'm able, I'll call back and have a look at him late afternoon.'

Julian came away from the window, his dark face sardonic, but he said nothing, just waiting patiently for the doctor to leave. If it was true, as they said, that the eyes revealed the self, young Dr Talbot had fallen madly in love at first sight.

CHAPTER FIVE

IT didn't take Charlotte very long to apologise. 'Forgive me, Fleur. I don't know what came over me.'

'I understand.'

'Yes, you do, don't you?' Charlotte's fine eyes softened into the ghost of a smile. 'Where did you learn it, Fleur? You were the same as a child.'

Matthew, to everyone's relief, rallied quickly, and Julian at least wasn't surprised when Dr Talbot found the time in his busy day to pay the patient another call.

'I like him,' Matthew said. 'I want him for my doctor from now on.'

'It couldn't have gone better if he'd planned it,' Julian was heard to observe very dryly, but as yet Fleur was quite unaware of her conquest.

The days slipped away and the morning before the party she plucked up the courage to put a suggestion to Charlotte.

'Why don't you get your hair cut?' she asked lightly as though she had just thought about it, instead of at least a couple of times every day.

'My hair?' Charlotte put down the morning paper and touched a hand to her heavy chignon.

'You've all got splendid hair,' Fleur pointed out sincerely. Only Charlotte's was pulled back tightly from her face, dragging out the natural curl.

'I'm too old to change my hair-style,' Charlotte said doggedly.

'A woman is never too old to change her hair-style,' Fleur said patiently. 'Anything that enhances a woman's personal confidence and well being is well worth thinking about. You know how much you liked *my* hair—well, I'm sure Glenn could fit you in.'

'But I'd feel naked without my hair!' Charlotte's expression was comical. 'It reaches almost to my waist.'

'It would be smarter, Aunt Charlotte, and it would make you look a whole lot younger. Most women would give anything to have thick, shining, naturally curly hair.'

'I'm nearly forty.'

'I'm not asking you to have a face-lift! Besides, the great beauties of the world are in their forties. Do let me ring Glenn. He'll make you feel and look so much better and we'll shop for a new dress.'

Some urge was on Charlotte, for after about an hour she told Fleur to ring up and see if she could make an appointment. As if we couldn't get in, Fleur thought to herself. Society put great store on the very wealthy and hairdressers depended on women who went to a great many social functions. Glenn would be only too pleased to see them and the appointments were made for mid-afternoon.

Glenn, on his mettle, went full out to effect a transformation. 'If you just step this way, Miss

Standford, I think we can surprise you.'

And stun them he did. With the great mane of yesterday swept away, Charlotte was overwhelmed by her unfamiliar reflection in the mirror.

'Congratulations, young man,' Charlotte said grandly, and actually smiled. 'I was so terribly nervous, but you've worked wonders.'

'If I might be permitted to say so,' Glenn, the guide to hundreds of women, stepped nearer the mirror, 'you look at least ten years younger.'

'I think I do.' Charlotte turned her head this way and that, revelling in the lightness of her head and the way a short, face-framing hair-style had such instant magic. Oh God, could it be possible! She was five feet nine in height, with such straight, determined features, yet she hardly recognised herself. Her thick black hair seemed pierced through with highlights, its deep waves and curls remarkably kind to her chiselled features. She had never noticed before that she had good eyes. Completely magnetised, she sat on, while Fleur felt within her a longing for Charlotte to shine. They had come all this distance, now they would get the dress.

'Are you ready, Fleur?' Charlotte finally stood up, entranced with herself and not knowing where it was going to end. If Kurt had found her attractive before, what would he think of her now? She was thirty-eight and no one had come along to liberate her yet.

To Fleur's pleased surprise, instead of having to coax Charlotte into the shops, there was no stopping her. Charlotte had subjugation on her mind and she didn't intend to bide her time.

It was Julian who put the finishing touch to Fleur's entrancing appearance.

'No one will be able to take their eyes off you,' Matthew announced, round-eyed. Ten minutes ago he had thought Fleur looked perfect in her lovely white chiffon gown; now for the first time in his young life he saw what jewellery was all about.

'Where did those come from, Uncle Julian?' He stared in awe at the emerald and diamond florette necklace around his sister's flawless young throat, then at the matching earrings that added such brilliance to her face.

'They were my mother's and they came to me for my wife.' Julian turned Fleur around so the two of them were reflected in the long triple mirror.

'Are you lending them to Fleur, then? What a shame!'

'Surely, Julian, I can wear something else?' Fleur said distractedly. The thought of Julian with a wife touched every raw nerve in her body.

'Look, darling, I'll lay it out for you,' Julian's dark voice was sardonic. 'I want you to look a vision, and you *do*.'

'Oh, my, yes!' Matthew smiled hugely. 'I expect Uncle Julian is trying to make Sheena jealous.'

'God help me, I never thought any such thing!' Julian walked away to the door, looking as if the whole world belonged to him. 'When you're ready,

Fleur, Grandfather would like to have a look at you. You, too, Matt, seeing you're making your debut.'

By eight o'clock nearly everyone had arrived, including Kurt Werner, who looked so unexpectedly at ease in evening clothes that Sir Charles, at first, did not recognise him.

'Who's the chap talking to Charlotte?' Sir Charles addressed Fleur in an undertone. He thought he knew everyone who was coming.

'Why, it's Kurt Werner!' Fleur told him in the same confidential tone.

'And who the devil asked *him*?' The handsome old face clouded with anger. More—outrage.

'*I* did,' Fleur answered quite calmly, and put a hand on his arm. 'You did tell me it was my party.'

'And this, miss, is *my* house. Since when have we included the gardeners on our guest list?'

'He's more than that, Sir Charles.' Fleur kept the luminous smile on her face. 'He has quite a successful business and he's turned your garden into a paradise.'

'I won't have Charlotte making a damn fool of herself! Where's her pride?'

'Look at them,' Fleur begged him. 'Really *look* at them. I'd say they make a very personable couple.'

'I'd say you've got too much to say for yourself altogether!' The old man gave her a fierce glare.

'Humiliate Charlotte,' Fleur told him quietly, 'and I'll walk out of this house tonight.'

'You won't, you know!' The fierceness died out of the blue eyes. 'And that's one hell of a way to blackmail me!'

'You know what they say, Sir Charles,' Fleur took a deep, long breath, 'all's fair in love and war.'

'Because Charlotte's in love?' he shot at her with obvious disbelief.

'I would say well on the way.' Fleur swallowed hard.

'Bah, she was born an old maid!' Sir Charles muttered, and stalked off to his friends.

With her chin tilted like a princess Fleur circled the reception rooms, conscious that everyone knew her background and speculated on her future. In a kind of mad defiance, Charlotte in a royal blue crêpe-de-chine that showed her splendid back snatched glass after glass of champagne off the trays, the unaccustomed alcohol boosting her confidence and loosening her tongue. It was, all in all, a kind of feverish evening.

Sheena kept close to Fleur as though in a short time they would be family anyway, though Fleur kept remembering how Sheena's mother's jaw had literally dropped open when they were introduced.

'On account of your red hair,' Sheena had explained away her mother's sheer amazement. Fleur herself had the uncomfortable notion that Mrs Lloyd had taken an instant dislike to her, but for what reason, she couldn't imagine. Maybe it was the admiration that was coming her way or the way the unpredictable Sir Charles insisted she play the piano for them and clapped loud and long when she was finished.

'Grandfather *is* in a good mood,' Charlotte whispered to Fleur, when she had been tense with worry. No one could say he had made a fuss of Kurt, neither had he ordered him straight out of the house. In her own way, Fleur had worked a revolution.

Immediately after supper, Matthew was sent to bed and Fleur walked up the stairs with him. 'You seemed to be enjoying yourself?'

'I actually had a glass of champagne.' Matthew burst out laughing.

'Only one, I hope!'

'All everyone is talking about is *you*,' Matthew told her. 'I'd say you were a huge success.'

'Didn't Lottie look nice?' Fleur took his arm.

'She's like another person with her different hair!' Matthew didn't even bother to stifle his yawns. 'I'll bet Grandad hits the roof when everyone goes home.'

'You're on!' Fleur felt the smile on her face.

'You mean you don't think he will?' Matthew looked relieved.

'It's quite apparent Mr Werner can hold his own. Besides, Julian was seen to be pleasant to him.'

'I do remember how it was before,' said Matthew. 'I hope it won't happen again. Poor old Lottie will grow her hair again, like a penance.'

The rest of the night passed very pleasantly and at the end, a whole lot of gratifying compliments, many of them sincere, Fleur thought, taking it all with a liberal pinch of salt.

'Well, I'm for bed,' Sir Charles announced after the last guest had gone. 'A very curious evening all round.'

Julian laughed, his blue eyes a dazzling colour against his darkly tanned skin. 'I enjoyed it very much.'

'So did I.' Charlotte, with a high flush in her cheeks, looked splendid and quite unlike herself.

'It's time we had a serious talk about that gardener feller!' Sir Charles shot his granddaughter an aggressive look. 'If there'd have been a policeman handy, I would have had him arrested on sight.'

'I think it's time for us all to turn in,' Julian said smoothly, getting a hand under his sister's elbow and assisting her to her feet.

'I meant what I said, Sir Charles,' Fleur whispered softly in the old man's ear.

'Did you, you little witch!' He put his arm around her narrow waist and kissed her on the cheek. 'If I've learnt something, you're one of the few people who's always stood up to me.'

'I expect you like it.' She smiled at him.

'I do.' Sir Charles paused to say goodnight and Charlotte watched him walk away with obvious relief.

'Dear me, I was terrified he would start, when I'm so desperately tired.'

'Go up to bed, then,' Julian told her. 'Fleur and I will lock up.'

'A lovely, lovely night!' Still brushed with happiness, Charlotte kissed both her brother and Fleur. 'I think I'll have a sleep-in in the morning.

For *once*.' She paused in the doorway and blew them another kiss.

'I—I hope——' Fleur wondered if she could even voice her hopes aloud.

'For a girl who's frightened of marriage you're doing your best as a matchmaker.' Julian sat down on a sofa and pulled her down beside him.

'But you know how Charlotte feels?' she answered him a little apologetically.

'No, not really—Charlotte has never confided in me.'

'She has so much, yet she's so vulnerable,' Fleur sighed.

'You forget we lost our parents when Charlotte, in particular, needed them most. Thirteen is a crucial age for a young girl. Our grandmother did everything she could, but Charlotte was always intimidated by the old man. David too.'

'Not you.'

'I could endure it, and he's got very many qualities to admire. Having too much power doesn't make anything easy, even for the one who has it.'

She sighed and tilted her head back, the emeralds glowing against her luminous white skin. 'Can any of us escape sorrow and bitterness?'

'It doesn't exist for *you* any more.'

The house was quite still. They were together, and deep within her, Fleur began to tremble. The long simmering hatred she had felt for Julian *had* to be kept alive; it was her only protection. Yet she was another person, unable to move away from him. It was like being in the lull of a storm, waiting for the lightning to strike.

He put his arm around her and turned her body to him. 'You're trembling.'

'Yes, by God!' she said with soft violence, the warring emotions showing in her eyes.

'You knew this was going to happen.'

She laughed a little wildly, very white, her green eyes blazing like a siren on a rock. 'You too, Julian, only you have a reason for everything you do.'

'Why not?' His eyes were very alert and intent on her.

'Then think about it again!' she cried contemptuously. 'I won't allow you to destroy me like you destroyed my mother.'

She tried desperately to obliterate excitement with anger, uncaring that his own anger was unleashed. He jerked her easily right across his knees, his hand under her chin, forcibly holding her glowing head up to him.

'Don't *touch* me, Julian!' Even as she spoke the words, her eyes were luring him on, her mouth anticipating the feel of his own.

'Do you think I don't know when a woman is leading me on?' His voice was steely with anger and something far stronger.

'All you have to do is let me go.'

'You've got a hell of a nerve to ask that!'

A finger of flame flickered deep in her body, gathered strength—a conflagration, with herself the victim. The situation was beyond her.

She gave an incoherent little cry, more seductive to the male than she would ever know, and Julian lowered his head, not crushing her into surrender but taking her mouth with passion and a consummate slow urgency.

She had nothing left—no pride, no resistance. The victory had been all too easy. The hurting hand under her chin moved to her hair, but still he didn't take his mouth from hers, nor did she attempt to turn her head away.

What price honour, moral fibre and a lifetime of disgust? He had set a trap for her to fall into which in itself was the lowest form of betrayal. Unsophisticated. A virgin.

He moved her closer into his arms, her capacity for sensuality driving him past the punishing kiss he had intended. His hand came down over her shoulder, under the flowery necklace that glittered so erotically, exploring the delicate bones. Her body was made for a man's delight; the skin so fine and dazzlingly white, small uptilted breasts that were now revealed in a deep semi-circle above the tight bodice of her dress.

His fingers burned across her sensitive skin, intent on inflicting the most exquisite pain.

'You don't know when to stop, do you?' she challenged him, while her body arched tautly with a will of its own. 'The one thing they never taught you!'

'What is written, is written,' he quoted in a voice that mocked them equally, while still sensuous beyond belief.

'I'll write my own fate, thank you. Not *you*!' Fleur whispered vehemently, the words ending in a strangled gasp as his hand slid down over her breast and captured it, delighting in its tender promise.

For an instant she was incapable of finding her voice and when she did, it shook badly. 'You have no right to touch me, Julian!' She caught at his wrist.

'But you love me.' His blue eyes blazed like the sky at midday.

'What are you *saying*?' She was visibly panicked, recoiling against his shoulder.

'A long time ago, you did,' he told her gently.

'Now I know how truly cruel you are.' She was scarcely aware her eyes were full of tears, silent, silver tears for the lost, loveless years. She *had* loved him, of course—idolised him, which made his fall from exhalted heights too bitter to be borne.

What was left was fascination; the terrible physical bond that still linked her so strongly to him. Her mind was chilled to ice, but her sorry, traitorous body was filled with a fire and audacity that would allow him to ruin her life.

'Poor little one. Poor flower-face.' He lifted his hand and with a gesture that could not deceive her, brushed away the shimmering tears. 'Don't cry!'

Her heart contracted at his tone. An actor's voice, to play upon the emotions. What an asset! 'I'm not going to let you jeopardise my little chance of happiness,' she told him with shaken turbulence.

'Because you're a child still, a frightened, bewildered child, bred on lies.'

'No, Julian. No more!' She made a determined attempt to lift herself out of his arms, but he held her so easily, infinitely stronger.

'It's a long time since you've let me cradle you in my arms,' he said softly. 'I thought I liked you best when you were round about five, but now I'm not at all certain.'

'You'll be certain of a vulgar scandal, if you don't let me go!'

His reaction to that was to laugh—a genuine laugh, full of soft amusement. 'You silly, bird-witted baby! Why, I've hardly touched you.'

'You've touched me where nobody else has,' she replied heatedly, then blushed deeply. Damn her rash tongue!

'Have I?' he brushed a kiss over her quivering mouth. 'I'm glad.'

'You should have been a sultan. And what about Sheena? Just how many women do you fit into your busy life?'

'As it happens, I'm only interested in one.' He pinned her flailing hands together and held them to his chest.

'Then I can't make much sense of what you're doing now.'

'Helping you grow up?' he offered helpfully, his blue eyes sparkling with insolence.

Her blood sang with fury. She wanted to kill him, but he held her hands. 'How kind! You should talk to Sheena about it—better yet, her mother. She took an instant dislike to me.'

'You're not the plainest little thing in the world,' he pointed out very dryly.

'And you're utterly untrustworthy—despicable! How can you hold up your head?'

'*How?*' he asked, mimicking her disparaging tone. 'Are you implying I'm wronging Sheena?'

'She can't possibly know what she's letting herself in for.'

'Surely you're not going to tell her?' Some primitive emotion prowled in his blue eyes, an inclination towards violence.

'Please, Julian, you're hurting me!'

'I want to!' He slid his arm under her back, half lifting her. She tried to cry out, expecting to be annihilated, but instead he tipped her head forward and released the catch on the necklace that sparkled so brilliantly around her throat.

'You really don't deserve such an honour. I'm keeping this for my wife.'

'You *brute*!' Her humiliation turned to scorn.

'That's just your view of my character.' Julian slid the necklace into his breast pocket with supreme unconcern.

'Don't forget the earrings.' Fleur tugged at her earlobes, wanting only to fling them at him.

'The earrings aren't important.'

'Oh yes, they are!' The hot blood was throbbing in her veins. 'You excel at this kind of thing, you rotten beast!'

There was a brilliant flash in his eyes, next thing he had flung her across his knees. She wanted to scream as his hand administered several hard slaps, but not a sound grazed her throat.

'You deserve that!' he told her unfeelingly, and finally turned her over again.

'You lily-livered thing!'

'You earned it,' he said hardly.

'Are you going to beat your *wife*?' she asked him passionately.

'Very likely.' His blue eyes swept over her, brilliant and ironic.

'Then I hope you end up in jail!'

'A pity you said that.' His hand twisted her head back into his shoulder and he kissed her with such violence she thought she would bear the imprint of his mouth for ever.

In fact, the slight swelling didn't take all that long to fade. When Fleur got up the next morning after a few hours dominated by savage dreams of Julian, it was gone. No questions would be asked, except the questions she asked her own heart.

To her equally intense relief and disappointment, Julian was called away for a week on business. Industrial disputes were threatening and it was expected of Julian to adroitly handle the situation before some of the central mines came to a halt. Sir Charles alternately cursed and became thoughtful or went off to the city to make plots of his own, and the rest of the world looked forward to Christmas.

The weather grew hotter, but Fleur had difficulty getting Charlotte's approval to take Matthew to the beach. There were glorious ocean beaches to the north and the south, drives of just over an hour, yet Charlotte remained fearful of what could happen.

'There's so much traffic on the highway. I know you're a good driver, but you haven't had all that much experience. What would happen if you broke down? Such a pretty girl and just a boy.'

'I think she's frightened of rapists,' Matthew confided later.

'Then we need a dog,' said Fleur.

'Gosh, you *have* got a determined little face!' Matthew sat back on the grass and stared at her. 'Is that what Uncle Julian calls ginger spunk?'

'Grandma Standford used to say that.' Fleur had to guard her expression just at the sound of his name.

'I heard Uncle Julian say it just the other day.' Matthew rolled over on his stomach. 'Anyway, this is supposed to be secret, but I'd better tell you now. Uncle Julian has placed an order for two pedigree collies. I love collies, don't you?'

'He's *what*?' Fleur burst out. She had intended going to the pound.

'He thought you might prefer a bitzer or an Irish wolfhound, but he said Grandfather had to be considered. Two pedigree pups or nothing. Grandfather might just understand.'

'So when are we getting them?' Fleur subsided, saying goodbye in her mind to two four-legged orphans.

'For Christmas.' Matthew turned back to his sister and smiled. 'It's all in the timing, Uncle Julian says. Don't forget, it's a secret.'

As it happened, Kurt hurdled the problem of getting them to the beach. While he worked on a miniature waterfall, Matthew told him all about Charlotte's fears.

'Could *I* not take you?' Kurt offered gravely. 'Miss Fleur could drive one way and I would drive the other. I'm sure all your aunt needs is reassurance. After all, your sister is a very capable young lady and you're a strong, big boy.'

'Getting there, anyway.' Matthew had gained almost seven pounds.

'If Miss Fleur is agreeable, I'll speak to your aunt this afternoon.'

'Oh, great! We haven't got Uncle Julian to help us, you see and no one bothers Grandfather.'

Kurt, who was well aware of Sir Charles' difficult temperament, characteristically said nothing to the boy, nor to the woman who occupied a good part of his thoughts. Their social equal he might never be in the old man's eyes, but he could, just possibly, offer friendship.

Charlotte was startled and pleased at Kurt's suggestion and enlisted Maria's willing aid in coming up with a picnic hamper to end all picnic occasions.

'I won't be swimming, though,' she told Fleur as though daring her to ask why.

'Why ever not?' Fleur asked, looking mystified. 'It's so hot!'

'If you must know, I'm shy. Or too modest.'

'What an excuse!' Fleur, slightly breathless from running up the stairs, collapsed into a chair. 'You've got a good figure. Show it off.'

'I'm a middle-aged woman.' There was a note of sadness in Charlotte's voice.

'So? You're looking terrific.' Briefly rested, Fleur jumped up. 'Where's your swimsuit?'

'Nothing like yours, miss, that leaves nothing to the imagination.'

'Good lord!' Fleur's bikinis, though brief, weren't particularly daring for the current trend. 'Pull it out,' she ordered.

Even while she argued, Charlotte went to a drawer in her wardrobe and retrieved a black, camisole-styled one-piece swimsuit. '*You* won't be able to sit out in the sun,' she told Fleur sternly, and held the swimsuit up.

'Very dashing!' said Fleur, visualising the swimsuit moulding Charlotte's tall, lean body. 'Poor old Kurt will go weak at the knees!'

The morning dawned brilliantly and they had a pleasant, uneventful trip to the south coast. Kurt drove, which seemed to make Charlotte happy, and Fleur and Matthew sat in the back seat singing snatches of songs along with Matthew's cassette recorder.

When they came on the blue, sparkling ocean, Fleur sat forward, staring out the window. 'Isn't it beautiful!'

'Beautiful indeed!' Kurt answered. 'I have never in all my wanderings around this world seen finer beaches than what we have here in Queensland. I am in love with your country.'

Charlotte flushed prettily and they parked the car near a quiet stretch of beach.

Hours slipped by and no one even spoke of going home. Matthew and Charlotte, with their olive skin, just turned a deeper shade of gold, but Kurt and Fleur kept strictly to the shade of the beach brolly once they were out of the water.

They had been sitting together in a companionable

silence, watching Charlotte and Matthew bobbing out in the water, when Kurt spoke his misgivings.

'I've so much enjoyed this day. I am, I suppose, a lonely man—solitary, you would say.'

'You speak as though you won't be joining us again.' Fleur turned to look at him, seeing how his blond hair fell softly across his brow. It made him look so much younger, even boyish.

'I think you know, Miss Fleur, it could cause unpleasantness in the home.'

'Please, call me Fleur.' She reached out and touched his hand. 'Forgive me, I don't mean to pry, but I think you have a special regard for Charlotte.'

'I do.' Kurt plunged his big hand into the white sand. 'I have tried to conceal it, but it is proving too strong for me. Then, little Fleur, you have made your own bid on my behalf. It was your idea to invite me to your party, was it not?'

'A very good idea,' she said quietly.

'You can't know what it cost me to come. I have experience of the so-called élite. Some of them can be very cruel, and none more than Charlotte's grandfather. He is a very arrogant man.'

'He's what life has made him.' Fleur stared out to sea.

'I'm afraid he would never accept me in any capacity other than the gardener.'

'And what is it you want?' she asked him as gently as possible.

'I would very much like to ask Charlotte's hand in marriage. I'm an old-fashioned man and Charlotte is very conscious of her duty to her grandfather. She would need his approval.'

'Have you spoken to her of this?' Fleur was a little astonished things had gone so far.

'No, no.' Kurt put his head in his two hands. 'Not only the grandfather but the money is the obstacle—too much money. A man must be master in his own home.'

'You mean you're jealous of Charlotte's money?'

'I have money of my own,' Kurt said with dignity. 'Not money as Charlotte is used to, but enough to keep a wife happy and comfortable. Then too, I have plans. In the ordinary way I would not be wasting my time coming every week to Waverley—only to see Charlotte. Such feeling we share was mutual from the very first day.'

'Don't forsake her, Kurt, because of a mistaken ideal. Charlotte hasn't known a great deal of love.'

'If I truly thought she was serious!' Kurt seemed to be drowning in doubt. 'Is it because she is so isolated? Men would fear to approach a goddess like that.' Fleur looked at him quickly, but it was entirely serious. 'She could help me so much with my work. My interests are hers—the wonderful discussions we have!'

'You must tell her how you feel.' Fleur was torn by a mad desire to laugh, though it was far from being a laughing matter.

'It would enrage the grandfather.'

Thoroughly, Fleur thought, but she said aloud: 'Charlotte has the right to lead her own life, to find happiness in her own home. Waverley goes to Julian on Sir Charles' death—I know this for a fact; Charlotte herself told me. Julian will marry and his wife will be mistress of the house, not Charlotte. Yet she loves it and has given her whole life to looking after her grandfather's interests.'

'If only she didn't have all that money,' Kurt muttered, his face twisted. 'The money is the worst part.'

'Is it *so* important?' Fleur asked abruptly, looking at his inflexible expression.

'I am afraid, yes.'

So Charlotte for the opposite reason risks another rejection, Fleur thought. Matthew ran up the beach and Fleur hopped up lightly and passed him a towel.

'That was great!' Matthew told them both enthusiastically. 'I think I'll ask Uncle Julian to get me a surfboard.'

Fleur drove home so competently, Charlotte in the back seat with Matthew became almost totally relaxed. With a driver always at her disposal Charlotte had never apparently considered taking to the wheel, though she had a good deal to say from the back seat.

'You should get your licence,' Fleur suggested, not bothered by the comments.

'A good idea!' Kurt looked over his shoulder to smile. 'The day might soon come when you will need to drive.'

Whatever Kurt meant, from the look on Charlotte's sun-flushed face it might have been a declaration.

'If you really think so, Kurt,' she said submissively, 'I'll consider it.'

CHAPTER SIX

As a result of the party at Waverley, Fleur received a good many invitations to parties and functions. She even received an invitation to a Sunday brunch and it was there she encountered Jon Talbot again. Not that their meeting had been left to chance. Her hostess, a young married, was Jon's second cousin, and when it was casually mentioned in passing that 'the Standford girl'—when of course she wasn't—had been invited, Jon had worked things so his name was taken off the weekend roster at the clinic. Eligible young bachelors were welcome everywhere and Jon had already privately confided to his cousin that 'he would sell his mother to the Arabs for a girl like Fleur!' Of course he wouldn't, being the apple of his mother's eye, but the point was well taken.

Fleur soon discovered she saw the same faces at the places she was invited, but she was quite unprepared to see Jon. Indeed, it took her a few lengthy seconds to place him, a fact which did nothing for Jon's usually buoyant self-confidence.

'Why, of course, Dr Talbot!' She gave him her hand.

'*Jon*, please.'

'Fleur,' she responded with a smile.

'I can't think of a name that would suit you

more.' With gentle determination he removed her to a relatively quiet corner. 'And how is the boy?'

'So well it almost seems like a miracle!' She looked at him with appeal in her widely spaced green eyes. 'Is this usual?'

'Well—' he hesitated, not liking to worry her; on the other hand it wouldn't be a kindness not to point out the facts—'this time of year we usually see a big reduction in cases. Spring is a bad time . . . winter. However, from what I've read up on your brother, his condition has been diagnosed as essentially emotional. Time will tell. There are established patterns. I've seen many children grow out of what was a chronic condition round about the age of fourteen, a kind of spontaneous remission.'

'Please God, Matthew will be one of them,' she said fervently.

He nodded sympathetically, sorry for the boy, but anxious to get on to a man-woman footing. Fleur looked like one of the brilliant little gazanias with her apricot head, creamy skin and bright yellow dress. He wasn't the only one who thought so, apparently, but none of them were to prove quite so determined.

Sheena and a male friend turned up about noon, Sheena particularly attractive in a sleeveless, high-slit white dress that made the most of the golden tan. There were cries of: 'Hi there!' all round, but Sheena spoke a few words to her tall, considerably older companion, then made directly for Fleur.

'How long have *you* been here?' she asked, smiling brightly. 'Hello there, Jon.' It was obvious she knew him and guessed Fleur's attraction, for her dark eyes narrowed wickedly. 'What did you *do* to get away from the clinic?'

'Worked beastly hard.' Jon smiled, but Fleur guessed correctly that Sheena not only had him placed firmly in the minor league, but Jon knew it.

'I've been meaning to ring you all week,' Sheena told Fleur with considerable charm, 'but business, business. I've had a colleague over from Paris.'

'Is that he?' Fleur glanced towards Sheena's companion, not young, not good-looking, but dressed in the height of fashion.

'Good heavens, no, darling!' Sheena burst out laughing. 'That's Clive Ashton of Ashton Associates. We've been very dear friends for years now.'

And that's all you'll ever be! Jon thought maliciously, but didn't say. Loaded Ashton might be, but macho he wasn't.

Evidently on the same train of thought, Sheena sighed: 'I wish to God Julian would come home! Nothing is the same without him.'

'He's expected back tomorrow,' Fleur offered consolingly, when she felt a vile wave of jealousy. The emotion shocked her so much she couldn't bear to analyse it.

'Yes, I know.' Sheena's abstracted tone implied that she had heard from Julian several times a day since he had been gone. 'I think he's got them where he wants them, don't you?'

'I really wouldn't know,' said Fleur, familiar

with the situation, but uncertain of its outcome.
Sir Charles had been very short-tempered and har-
assed, very much against the trade unions' demands, in his view, at the expense of the economy.

'At least he's not a typical boss,' Jon made the
startling observation.

'Julian?' Sheena looked at him sharply as
though he had implied a criticism.

'Yes, of course,' Jon answered simply. 'That's
why he's listened to. He's shown over and over
that he's a very reasonable man but plenty tough
enough at the right time. Actually it's a good thing
he's around to put the brakes on Sir Charles—
there's a boss if you want one!'

'How do you think he's got where he is today?'
Sheena asked aggressively.

'Ah, but it doesn't work any more.' Jon shook
his head. 'Anyway, let's talk about something else,
not industrial conflicts.'

'What a good idea!' Fleur stepped between
them. 'I'd love another cup of coffee.'

'Clive!' Sheena put up her hand and waggled her
fingers.

Clive Ashton excused himself from his little
group and started towards them.

'Clive's in the rag trade among other things,'
Sheena put a friendly hand on Fleur's arm. 'I'd
like you to meet him.'

By now it was a terrible crush and Fleur rather
longed to go home. Instead she felt obliged to stay
on for another hour, chatting a whole lot about
nothing, until at long last Jon walked with her to

her car.

'*Must* you race away?' his attractive, easy-going face looked crestfallen.

'I promised Matthew I'd give him a game of tennis.'

'You *are* a devoted sister,' he commented.

'I am.' She looked up and smiled at him. 'If you've nothing better to do, you might like a game?'

'Yes, ma'am,' he smiled back, dazed she had invited him.

'See you about three, then.' Jon held the door and she got into her car.

'Just tell me how well you want me to play?'

'I think I can surprise you,' she said, and drove away.

In the end, it nearly turned into a tournament because Charlotte, an excellent player, thought she needed the exercise and Matthew, pleased and excited, got on the phone and invited two of his friends.

'Are you ready, boys?' Charlotte called to them in the first game of doubles, and got right behind her serve.

'Ready, Lottie,' Matthew answered from the sidelines, and sat back to have a good laugh. The friends he had called would have exhausted most adults and Simon, the under-fifteen school champion, hammered Charlotte's service back.

'Wow!' Jon, who had just arrived, sat down beside Matthew.

'Simon's an old hand at this sort of thing,' Matthew told him, giggling. 'Did you ever see anything funnier than Lottie's face?'

Fleur waved, wanting only a relaxing game, but Charlotte, put on her mettle, flexed her knees. She was somewhat surprised at that excellent return of service, but most probably it was a fluke.

It wasn't, and because the boys didn't play in the least like little gentlemen the score came out six-three in favour of the boys.

It was a far more enjoyable afternoon than it had been that morning and Maria came out beaming expansively with lemonade and cakes for the boys and tea or coffee for the adults.

Some time after five, Charlotte organised Adams to drive the boys home and Matthew went along for the ride. Left on their own, Fleur and Jon relaxed in the garden chairs laughing at all the amusing things the boys had said.

'You really like children, don't you?' Jon's eyes softened as he looked at Fleur's lovely, softly flushed face.

'Doesn't everybody?' Her green eyes were brilliant with contentment. 'Of course he picked on the very best players he could think of, the little beggar.'

'All he needs is a little coaching himself.' Jon was serious for a moment. 'It's remarkable, the effect of the mind on the body. As a doctor, I don't believe in faith healers, at the same time I recognise the powerful effects of the mind over the body. Even in the short time I've known him, Matthew looks a different boy.'

'Yes, he's well and he's happy.' Fleur's smile was full of love for her brother, but Jon preferred to interpret it as a deep pleasure in his company. He put out his hand and covered hers on the table.

Fleur blinked, a little astounded at the ardency of the pressure, and as she straightened, she saw Julian dressed casually in beige slacks and a soft pull-on cotton shirt cross the lawn and come towards them. Innocent as she was, she felt as though she had been caught in an illicit relationship.

'How's it going?' His blue eyes looked blandly from one to the other.

'Standford, how are you?' Jon jumped to his feet.

The two men shook hands as men will while Fleur tried to quiet her thumping heart. Instant chemistry, that's what it was. Once she understood it, she could pull out of her dilemma.

'We didn't expect you until tomorrow, Julian.' She didn't realise it, but she was looking into his face as though it concealed the secret to her whole life. What were his motives for making love to her? To make her suffer more?

'I persuaded myself I could do no more. At least the atmosphere is a whole lot more conducive to sensible discussion.'

Jon immediately asked a few intelligent questions and Fleur sat back wondering what it was about Julian that drew her like a magnet. It wasn't looks alone; not every handsome man had a sexual aura. Was it the mind behind the face? The brilli-

ance that showed through the eyes. He had such
alive eyes, whether they rested on a woman or not.
She had endured so much because of Julian. He
was her enemy, not her friend.

The men were still talking, unaware of her close
regard. Jon was an attractive man and he appeared
to like her, yet it didn't seem at all possible she
could become involved with him. Maybe she
should try; to persuade herself that Julian could be
easily expurgated. Her emotions were founded on
those of a child, an impressionable little girl. What
kind of a man was Julian to love?

He chose that precise moment to turn and add-
ress her, and his eyes narrowed at the expression
on her face.

'Snap out of it, darling.' For an instant they sat
there assessing one another like long-time oppo-
nents and Jon gave a little embarrassed cough.

'Well, I've had a very enjoyable afternoon, but I
must be gone.' He wavered a little as though
someone would ask him to tea, but it was clear
there was an unexpected current of hostility float-
ing around.

'Come again.' Fleur stood up, very small by
Julian's shoulder.

'I'd like that.' It was not the time to ask her out
to dinner, but Jon looked beyond the odd moment
to tomorrow. Something about the situation
eluded him and he wanted time to think about it.
Clearly little Fleur and Standford were antago-
nists. What was wrong?

They both saw Jon to his car and when Fleur

went to slip away, Julian caught her by the wrist.

'You're not going to cure yourself with the doctor.'

'Let's say I'm going to try.' It was useless to pretend he couldn't read her mind. They both knew it.

'I won't let you,' he said quietly, and pressed his thumb into her pulse. 'What you're thinking of is serious. The poor devil fell in love with you when he was supposed to be helping Matthew.'

'He *did* help Matthew,' she said stubbornly.

'It wouldn't be a kindness, would it, to encourage him?' Julian looked down at her glowing titian head. 'Already he senses something wrong, but he doesn't know what it is.'

'And what *is* it?' She swung around to face him, throwing her head back because he was so much bigger and so damned arrogant it was unbelieveable.

'You belong to me,' he said, and drew her towards him with infinite grace.

'That was yesterday!' she shook her head wildly. 'That was the time I believed in you.'

'I haven't changed.'

'No,' she said violently. 'But *I* have!' Perhaps her body might burn, but her vision remained clear. 'I've weighed you up and found you desperately wanting.'

'You feel things very deeply, don't you, Fleur?' Julian didn't seem angry at all but faintly weary.

She shrugged her shoulders impatiently, unwillingly leaning back against his locked arms. 'It's your pride that wants to keep me your slave.'

'Whatever it is,' he released her abruptly, 'just take my word for it, it's no go with the doctor.'

'Do you really think so?' She deliberately threw him a look of challenge. 'I found him sort of attractive . . . you know . . . decent.'

She saw his face change and took instantly to her heels. It was dangerous to provoke him; why did she do it?' ¬

The trees overhead were a canopy of dense leaves and blossoming oleanders six feet high all but fenced off the drive. It was a tumult of perfume and colour, and Fleur had had much too much sun.

Fleeing towards the drive, she didn't even notice the Rolls turn quietly at the magnificent wrought iron gates and then cruise up the drive. She was blind to everything, anyone, anything, but Julian. It wasn't until the powerful, big car was looming on her that she saw it and tried to skid to a shuddering stop.

She heard the brakes screech, saw Adams' agonised face, then Julian's arm was around her and he literally threw them both off the path.

She fell heavily, but stirred quickly, moaning. Julian said nothing at all. He was lying perfectly still, his eyes closed and his long, lean body slumped.

'*Julian!*' she exclaimed, in an excited, frightened voice. She rose on her knees and stared down at him. So many emotions filled her mind and an intense anguish. He had deliberately put himself in danger. 'Oh, Julian,' she said, and fell across him, her head pressed against his heart.

'A strange reaction for a girl who hates me,' he suddenly said above her, his voice clipped.

Very slowly she sat up and stared at him. '*More* games?'

'The danger was real enough, you little fool!'

Adams was upon them, and Matthew, both calling sharply: 'Are you all right?'

Julian sat up and shook his head. 'I won't know until I have a closer look.'

'I never thought for a moment. . . .'

'It's all right, Des,' Julian interrupted the distraught chauffeur.

'It's my fault entirely,' Fleur told them. 'I was acting crazily.'

'Have you hit your head, Uncle Julian?' Matthew asked, his voice low and anxious.

'I'm O.K.!' Julian put out his hand and rubbed his nephew's tense face.

'Fleur owes you one,' Matthew said solemnly. 'We were coming pretty fast.'

'Well, there's not a scratch on either of us,' Julian said calmly. He glanced at Fleur, whose red-gold curls were clinging damply to her forehead, then got an arm around her and raised them both to their feet.

'Let me take you up to the house in the car,' offered Adams, still in a state of shock.

'An offer we can't refuse.' Julian still had his arm around Fleur.

'Are you all right, Fleur?' Matthew's blue eyes

widened in alarm.

'She's O.K.,' Julian told him, doing all the talking. 'Open the door for us, like a good boy.'

'Honestly, I was scared stiff!' Matthew jumped to obey. 'So was Des. Considering you only had a minute, Uncle Julian. . . .' he tried to laugh.

'I'm sorry, Matt.' Fleur began to cry.

'Stop that!' Julian responded by picking her up in his arms.

'I acted like a fool.' Her control was slipping and she turned her head into Julian's shoulder.

'Brandy is always good for shock,' Matthew announced.

'Where did you learn that?' Julian smiled at him, his calm manner reassuring.

'Maria. She's always got it handy.'

There was a long silence and Des Adams laughed. 'A secret vice uncovered!'

'I don't give a damn as long as she always has dinner ready.' Julian, quite recovered, seemed amused. He put Fleur into the back seat and got in beside her. 'There's a conspiracy going on to keep us together in the back seat of a Rolls.'

She took a long, deep shuddering breath, but she couldn't answer. She was blaming herself for having drawn him into danger.

In the following week, a settlement was reached between mine owners and employees and Julian appeared on national T.V. looking, as Sheena put it, more like a sex symbol than the representative of big business. That was until he opened his mouth, Fleur considered. Then he was all mining magnate, highly articulate and persuasive and a brilliant mining engineer in his own right.

Sir Charles sat glued to the set for the entire time that Julian was on and afterwards muttered fiercely as he did when he was moved: 'Richard would be proud of him. Richard, my son!'

In a piercing moment Fleur glimpsed the desolation in the old man's eyes, and immediately she slipped out of her chair and went to sit at his feet, grasping his hand.

They looked at one another for a moment in silence, then Sir Charles stroked her hair. 'You're a good girl, Fleur, and you'll make a fine woman. Sweet and compassionate, like my Sarah.'

Life went on. With the advent of the festive season entertaining and being entertained was high on the agenda. As Fleur expected, Jon Talbot rang and, hell bent on defying Julian, she accepted every one of his invitations; and not only his. She was young, very pretty, and she soon came to see she could spend every night of the week out if she wished. But of course she didn't. Her greatest pleasure was being with her brother, for she counted his happiness above her own.

She soon learnt that the whole household loved music, from Sir Charles down to Maria, so the beautiful Steinway grand got played frequently. Sometimes the old man came into the room and sat quietly for an hour. Other times he sat beside her on the long ebony seat and played a few crashing chords of his own, pleasure and amusement on his autocratic face. Even Charlotte seemed content, so it was to be expected her grandfather thought she needed a timely jolt.

One evening when Fleur and Matthew were playing chess in the library and Julian was working quietly at his desk, Sir Charles came to the door, his thick, still black eyebrows working.

'Charlotte is on the phone to that damned gardener feller. From the sound of her voice I'd say she was going bonkers.'

Julian, intent on his work, looked up with almost total disinterest, but Fleur was alarmed by the acid tone.

'Please, Grandfather——' it just slipped out when she always called him Sir Charles—'Charlotte really likes him and he cares deeply about her.'

'Bunkum!' the old man retorted rudely.

'Because it's not what you like to hear?'

Their eyes met knowingly and he made an impatient gesture. 'Now, now, don't start standing up to me!'

Matthew's hand on the pawn trembled and Fleur caught his fingers. 'If you only got to know him, Sir Charles . . .'

'*Grandfather's* fine!' Momentarily the old man seemed nonplussed. 'How's it coming, Julian?'

'It's all in the interpretation.'

'Oh, well, you're the expert there. What about Charlotte, now? What do you think?'

'Leave well alone.' Julian seemed determined to get back to his work, his dark face faintly remote and unyielding.

'So you two are in cahoots, then?' For some reason this appeared to ease the old man's mind. 'You always were,' he maintained, and stomped away.

It was Matthew's turn to be curious. 'What does cahoots mean?' he enquired.

'It means,' said Julian, 'we agree about Charlotte, if nothing else.' As he spoke, there was an ironic twist to his mouth and he looked at Fleur deliberately, always searching for the gap in her guard.

She wasn't going to allow him that luxury. He knew far too much about her already. 'Please, Julian, may we have a Christmas tree?' she asked sweetly.

'Oh, let's!' Matthew begged. 'We haven't had one up since Grandma died.'

'Then ring up for one in the morning,' said Julian, and returned to his papers. 'No, hang on, I'm sure there's one up in the attic.'

'Not the one that used to reach to the ceiling?' Fleur's eyes shone as a vision drifted into her mind, a great tree hung with hundreds of glittering baubles and a five-pointed star at the top.

'I think so.' Julian put his arms behind his head, then stretched languidly like a sleek cat. 'I suppose I won't get any peace until we see it.'

Recognising the indulgent note in his uncle's voice, Matthew jumped to his feet. 'Great! Let's go up now.'

'Coming, flower-face?' Julian got up, smiling mockingly.

The most perverse reason made Fleur stay in her chair until he took her hand, so it pained her and excited her too the way her fingers curled into his own. She really needed a psychiatrist to analyse her— her whole life. His hand tightened and she looked up at him, a terrible awareness in her green eyes.

'How is Jon?' he asked suavely.

'I won't tell you.' She made a futile effort to pull away. Trust him to ask a totally irritating question—and at *that* time!

'It must be very flattering to be so much in demand,' he added.

'If you ask me,' said Matthew, 'he's absolutely mad about her!'

'You don't sound happy?' At some note in Matthew's voice, Fleur looked at him worriedly.

'He's all right,' said Matthew with affected unconcern, 'but he's so ordinary, isn't he, compared to Uncle Julian. They all are.'

'That's my boy!' Julian turned to his young nephew and smiled. 'I don't even believe it's basic prejudice.'

'*I* do!' Fleur told him scornfully, but she took great care not to look up into his blue eyes.

CHAPTER SEVEN

THEY had a very big party on Christmas Eve, more than a hundred people, and the house was a mass of shifting people. There was music and laughter and plenty of good conversation and, outside on the rear terrace and huge informal entertainment area, dancing for the younger guests.

Fleur wore a long, thin strapped petticoat of green chiffon and its beautiful clinging cut made her look incredibly slender and fragile. With it she wore the emerald and diamond earrings, for Julian never had taken them back, and they looked absolutely perfect.

Of course she had asked Jon, but she was a little wary now of the depth of his attentions. They danced frequently and each time he held her a little closer, more possessively, his blue-green eyes telling her what she didn't want to know. He was in love with her, after all, so she shouldn't be so surprised.

From the crowd around Julian, he was the most amusing, most intelligent and easily the best looking man in the place. Whenever he looked Fleur's way, she looked away. She didn't really care to see Sheena almost draped over his arm, her scarlet silk jersey dress worn the wrong way round in Fleur's opinion. It was perfectly in order for a woman to show off a pretty bosom, but not to *that* degree.

Jon's voice said in her ear: 'You look exquisite

tonight. No one could wear a dress like that unless they were young and perfect.'

She smiled at him a little abstractedly and never stopped to question whether it was wise. Over the moving dancers' heads she saw Julian and Sheena take the floor, Sheena giving him a brilliant smile. Knowing looks followed them, nods and smiles.

'What are you thinking about?' Jon asked in surprise.

'Oh, nothing, really!'

'You looked upset, disturbed.' He stared straight down into her cameo face.

'*Did* I?' She made a great effort to smile brightly. 'Sorry. It's just that you might be holding me that tiny bit tightly.'

'Oh——' Jon relaxed his hold a fraction, 'I keep forgetting what a fragile little thing you are.'

Later he danced her into the shadows and his arms tightened determinedly round her. 'I think I've fallen in love with you, Fleur,' he murmured in a voice she hadn't heard from him before.

'But I don't know, Jon.' She didn't want to hurt him, but she had to. 'I don't want to love anyone.'

'What's happened to you? Why are you frightened?' He was quickly losing his head, desperate to kiss her. She was twisting his heart, this strange little girl with her mixture of vivacity, sadness and intrigue.

'What *is* love?' she sighed. 'What is so different about me?' She felt depression pouring over her. In the middle of gaiety and laughter with a man who had actually told her he was in love with her, she wanted to cry.

It was too much for Jon. She didn't realise it, but sadness pointed up her looks. She was just a baby with scars.

He drew her ardently into his arms, half crazy with longing, touching her mouth at first lightly with his own, then shaken by desire, hard and searching.

'No! Stop!' She pushed back frantically. She wanted no one to touch her but Julian. He possessed her completely, coming between her and every other man. Jon was just a shadow, his seeking mouth without the power to move.

'I'm a fool—you're not ready.' Jon cursed himself bitterly. 'Forgive me, Fleur, but it's difficult to treat you like porcelain when you're such a desirable woman.' But repressed, he diagnosed, desperately shy and repressed. One didn't encounter it often enough. He had badly blundered. 'Let's go back,' he said lightly, and let her go. 'I'll get you a nice cold drink.' Fleur gave a curious little sigh and he took her arm as if she were a child. 'Just to be sure of it, I want to tell you my intentions are entirely honourable.' Probably for the first time in my life, he thought wryly.

Fortunately she laughed. 'Don't be angry with me. I do really enjoy your company.'

It would have to do. Jon left her in the scented coolness of the terrace and went indoors to get them both a drink.

Trailing flowers from a hanging basket brushed her shoulder and she turned her head to drink in the sweet elusive perfume. Her heart was beating in a very odd place, somewhere near her throat.

'Come on,' said Julian behind her in a terse voice, and took hold of her bare arm.

She didn't resist, exultant in having drawn him to her side, for whatever reason.

'Just as I told you, your doctor friend is becoming deadly serious,' he told her crisply.

'Yes, he is.' She seized on the fact with a crazy abandon. Don't let him think he was the only man who could awaken her to life.

'Do you *want* to hurt him?' he demanded. 'Why?'

'Perhaps I'm like my mother.' The thought came to her so bitterly she said it.

'I'd kill you if you were!' He flashed her a glance full of a terrifying anger.

'Anyway, it's *my* affair.' There had been no calculation in her dismal remark. She was off balance, heading towards disaster.

There were people seated, standing, everywhere and best irony of all, Julian had to keep smiling, answering the occasional called remark. It was all so very civilised, but Fleur knew she would have a bruise on her arm.

'What are you going to do with me?' she asked with a shaky laugh.

'Throw you in the lake.'

'Surely that's not the *only* way to get rid of me? I mean, you managed it before.' She knew she was going crazy, yet there was excitement and spice in it.

'If you had the least bit of sense you'd stop now.' They were isolated now, the clash of their voices beyond the range of curious ears.

'It's Christmas,' she reminded him sweetly.

'Where's your Christmas spirit?'

'It's probably time I gave you another spanking.'

'Dear Julian! Always the disciplinarian.' She could smell the fragrance of the flowers all around them. It was a delight and an anguish.

'Careful,' he warned, and she could see the tension in his body. 'Remember who you are and where you are.'

'For God's sake, I've had enough of the Standfords!' So many emotions exploded in her head—anger, humiliation, a white-hot, headlong yearning. She wanted him to pull her into his arms and crush her. She wanted him to force the very heart from her body.

But he did not. 'Some time, Fleur, these people are going to go home.' His blue eyes slashed to her trembling mouth. 'Who's going to protect you then?'

'Oh, I'll drag in someone,' she promised. 'Sheena.'

'You're quite crazy.' He looked at her with the distaste an adult shows for a childish tantrum.

'Good grief, she's checking on us now!' Fleur turned and looked away across the velvety expanse of grass. 'You'd better watch it if you don't want to lose her.'

'Oh, there you are!' Sheena called. 'Jon's getting so concerned about you, Fleur.'

Champagne glass still in her long narrow hand, Sheena covered the distance between them, gazing sharply from one to the other. 'Surely you're not having an argument?' she asked in a teasing voice that still held a hint of strain in it.

'More or less,' Fleur answered quite jauntily. Her green eyes were glittering like emeralds and her white skin was shot through with pulsating colour.

'*Oh!*' Sheena's voice changed again, full of concern and apparent dismay. 'Couldn't I arbitrate?'

'Whose side are you on?' Fleur began to laugh.

'I've got a feeling you've had a teensy-weensy bit too much of champagne,' Sheena murmured teasingly in tones that sounded remarkably patronising.

'You could be right.' Fleur didn't allow herself to show the faintest trace of anger. 'I haven't had your amount of practice.'

'Well, really!' Sheena looked considerably taken back, but Julian, unexpectedly, gave a brief laugh.

'As co-host with my grandfather I'm obliged to go back inside,' he said.

'I agree.' Fleur clapped delicately. 'Don't let me detain you.'

Sheena's eyes narrowed and her nostrils quivered like a pointer on the trail. She was madly, fiercely in love with Julian and she had metaphorically clawed more than one rival to bits; now she was faced with the most incredible contretemps of her life. Impossible as it would have seemed, Julian had some interest in this little redheaded minx from his past. The thought so disturbed her she didn't touch a bite of supper, and when the magnificent old grandfather clock in the entrance hall chimed twelve o'clock, she forcibly pulled Julian's elegant raven head down to her and in full view of at least forty highly interested guests kissed him lingeringly on the mouth. It was public knowledge, wasn't it, that she had lasted longer than most of Julian's women friends? She had boasted of it everywhere. Now she would have to work on the little cousin, poor relation—no damned relation whatever. She didn't trust Fleur one little bit.

It was two o'clock before the last guest went home and eight o'clock in the morning before Matthew could contain himself no longer. He padded along to Fleur's room and found her fast asleep, her head fiery against the lace-trimmed pillow, one arm flung away to the other side of the huge fourposter bed, the other dangling over the side towards the new, palest green carpet. It was a lovely room now, full of light and sensual charm. It had been the greatest joy helping Fleur change things. Uncle Julian had supplied the painting—Portrait of a Lady—by the French painter Jacques Emile-Blanche, and its subtle opulence and panache pointed up the delicate luxury of the room.

Fleur still slept and Matthew hesitated now wondering whether to wake her. She didn't look particularly happy. She even looked as though she might have been crying in her sleep. Maybe she had stayed up dancing until four o'clock in the morning, when he had had one of the best nights' sleep he had ever had.

'Fleur.' Very gently he pressed a spot behind her ear. He had never actually found out if this was indeed the best way to wake people out of a deep sleep.

'Hmmmmm?' She stirred, but her eyes were still tightly closed.

'Do wake up! It's absolutely the most super day and you can hardly see the tree for the presents.'

It took another minute of blandishments before Fleur opened her eyes. Then she saw her brother's thin, tanned face and his blue, blue eyes, and her own eyes stung with sudden tears.

'Hello there. Happy Christmas!'

'Happy Christmas!' Matthew's young voice sounded a little hoarse with emotion, then he bent down and gave her a resounding kiss on the cheek. 'Do get up.'

'But I'm dead beat.'

'Well, you can go back to bed after lunch.'

'Thanks a lot!' It was Christmas Day and she didn't feel she could face it.

'Do you suppose Uncle Julian remembered about the collies?' asked Matthew.

'Of course he did.' Fleur discarded all thoughts of lying around in bed. 'Julian never forgets anything vital. Or anything else for that matter.'

'How nice of you to say so!' Julian himself responded from the open doorway.

'Oh, hi, Uncle Julian!' Matthew went to him and Julian put his arm about the boy's shoulder. 'Happy Christmas.'

'Happy Christmas to you, too, Matthew,' said Julian. 'If you want to know where at least two of your presents are, go and find Des.'

'You beauty!' Matthew cried, and laughed in anticipation. 'Don't go away, I'll be right back.'

He ran away and Fleur drew in her breath deeply. She was still sitting up in bed and wore only her pink satin nightie. Her eyebrows lifted. 'I think you should go away,' she said.

'I like you in pink,' said Julian. 'It suits you.'

There was a wonderful, sleek glossiness about him this morning. Eyes, hair and skin shone with health and vitality. He was wearing a short-sleeved blue cotton shirt and against it his deeper coloured blue sapphire eyes looked dazzling.

'Happy Christmas,' he said with more mockery than sincerity.

' 'Bye, Julian,' she said, and pushed back against the mound of pillows.

'You can't be serious!'

'Oh, but I am.' The thin strap of her nightdress fell off her shoulder and she pushed it back up with a look of irritation. He would be able to see the shape of her clearly, but she refused to clutch hysterically at the top sheet.

'Is it really the same girl who went too far last night?' He came away from leaning against the door and crossed over to the bed.

'I'm warning you, Julian!' Her green eyes were enormous but still full of courage.

'I don't really take an awful lot of notice of your warnings.'

'Matthew will be back in a moment.'

'It will take him longer than that. There are a few things Des will want to explain to him. Then too Des and his wife have a present for him. Maria will probably waylay him as well.' He sat down on the side of the bed, put out a hand and tossed her hair. 'What's happened to all the ginger spunk?'

'I'm very conventional in my thinking,' she said coolly, her eyes going beyond him to the door now only slightly ajar. Help. Rescue. It was shocking to have Julian beside her like this when she had dreamt him there in the hours before dawn.

'I've got something for you,' he told her soothingly. 'Among other things.' He put his hand into his breast pocket and withdrew a cascade of white and green fire. 'You look surprised.'

Something started to ache at the base of her throat and she pressed a hand to it. 'You're not going to fasten that on me!' she protested.

'Aren't I?' He smiled a little tautly at her tone. 'It's beautiful, isn't it? It matches your eyes.'

'I'm sure you told me you were keeping it for your *wife*.'

'I'm equally sure my future wife will approve.'

'Then you don't know your sweet little Sheena!' She swung her small feet out of the bed. 'She was looking at me last night like a wild jungle tigress.'

'I noticed that myself.' Julian flickered her a satirical smile. 'Can't we possibly be friends, Fleur, just for the day?'

'Go away!' Sunlight fell across her hair and it glittered and danced like segments of living flame.

For answer he slipped the necklace around her throat and secured the clasp. 'Perhaps you can keep it for a rainy day.'

The mocking indulgence in his face desperately antagonised her. '*Doctors* do pretty well, I'm told.'

He moved so swiftly she could scarcely credit she was lying down again and he was leaning over her.

'What did you expect?' he asked crisply.

'You love flinging me around! It makes you feel

good.' She sat up precipitously, the furious light in her eyes dying abruptly as he put his hands on her narrow waist.

'*Don't*, Julian!' she protested.

'I'm inclined to agree.' There was a note of edgy sensuality in his voice.

'Then give it up.' She jerked her head back distractedly. 'We're enemies, you know.'

'Only my hands won't do the hating.' He lifted them slowly over her and cupped her tender young breasts. The small, rosy nipples were clearly visible through the thin material, taut with arousal.

'I'll fight you to the last inch!' The blood was glittering like fire in her veins, but she forced her body to go rigid in protest. Rigid, that was, until his thumbs stroked the tightly budded nipples, then desire flared in her such as she had never been prepared for in her life. Oh God, how he knew how to make her suffer!

She swayed towards him involuntarily, feeling such frightening flutters of pleasure, her eyes closed against the rapture.

'Trust me, flower-face,' he breathed against her parted lips.

'*Never!*' She meant it even as she was in the grip of a racking passion.

It wasn't enough to be kissed. Her woman's body demanded, needed so much more. She felt overburdened with her single flimsy garment, equally grateful she had it lest she surrender herself entirely.

'*God!*'

It didn't sound like Julian's voice at all; a

shaken breath of sound, not cool and masterful.

It should have been golden nectar itself to her such momentary conquest, but Fleur was too bedazzled herself to feel the triumph. She was alive as she had never been before and it was an agony, exquisite. His mouth came back to hers again, warm and beautiful and so very sure. She pulled him down with her on to the bed, careless of everything except this living temple of fire.

He broke away from her with soft violence, holding her with one hand, his voice a little harsh as though he forced himself to say the single word. '*No!* It's impossible, Fleur.'

Of course he was right, and immediately she was ashamed. She flung herself over so her head was buried in the pillows, her whole slender body shuddering with frustration. 'Why do you *do* things like this?' she accused him.

'Because I want you.' He lifted her bodily then and set her down on the floor.

'For how long?' She couldn't even stand without his support.

'Until I change.'

'That's the truth!' She choked on his unbearable cynicism.

'Why don't I put you under the shower?' His eyes rested on her dazed face and quivering limbs.

'Don't try it—I'll try to drown you.'

'You have to get dressed, darling. You can leave it though, if you want.'

'I hope something terrible happens to you, Julian.' She stared up at him with trancelike concentration.

'It already has.' Mockery touched his cleanly defined mouth. 'Now would you like me to run the cold water?'

'I'd like you to *get out*!' Anger whipped strength into her boneless limbs.

He smiled at her and dropped a final, careless kiss on her outraged mouth. 'Don't forget to take the necklace off.'

'I won't!' she promised him wrathfully. 'I'm going to leave it there until Sheena and her dear mother come. I'm going to tell them you put it there and I'm going to tell them *when*!'

His blue eyes swept over her like an intolerable stimulant. 'And don't forget to tell them you've been trying to seduce me since you were four years old.'

'So what happened to you?' she asked him with passionate vehemence. 'Cold feet?'

'It won't hurt either of us to bide our time.' He moved to the door, all arrogant masculinity, and Fleur threw the pillow.

'You're rotten, Julian. Absolutely rotten!'

'But I know *you*!'

Of course the pillow missed him. He picked it up off the floor with one graceful movement and threw it with perfect precision towards the head of the bed.

'Cheer up, darling,' he said dryly. 'You have to get used to dealing with dishonourable intentions.'

'I can well believe it, living here with *you*!'

'Touché!' He gave a warm, dry laugh, then disappeared through the door.

*

Sheena, at home, got busy on her mother to remember everything she could about the notorious Helena.

'Please, Ma,' she said. 'There's a powerful story there somewhere.'

Mrs Lloyd did her very best to oblige. She had great expectations for her daughter and she had been given to understand, as well as the evidence of her own eyes, that Fleur posed a threat. I mean, where had the girl come from originally? she thought. There was no talk of a father. Perhaps Helena had never been married at all before she met David Standford. Perhaps she was *worse*? It appeared to be Sheena's and her mother's job to find out.

True to tradition, Charlotte and her grandfather had words on Boxing Day. The upshot was that Charlotte retired and having upset the household Sir Charles went off well pleased. He was, Fleur considered, a terrible old man, a born troublemaker, never happier than when everyone and everything around him was seething. The only thing that saved him was that when one felt justified in murdering him he did an about-face and showed flashes of great charm.

Fleur hesitated outside Charlotte's bedroom door, not wanting to intrude and not wanting to leave Charlotte alone either, then she knocked.

There was no answer, and as Fleur pressed her ear to the door, no sound at all. For an instant she felt stricken, then she considered Charlotte wasn't the sort of person to hang herself from the rafters.

'Charlotte,' she called quietly. Charlotte had

told her to drop the 'aunt'.

There was a sound at last. A sob.

Fleur opened the door with decision and went in. She imagined Charlotte would be lying crumpled on the bed, but Charlotte had too much backbone for that. She was packing.

'What are you doing?' Fleur looked her dismay.

'I'm putting clothes in a bag.'

'He didn't mean it, Charlotte.' Fleur sank down on the bed.

'Oh, yes, he did!' Charlotte strode away to the bureau. 'To think I've given him my life and all it's made him do is despise me!'

'But he's just a terrible little boy.'

'Actually he's eighty years old.' In her haste, Charlotte was dropping underwear all over the floor.

'You can't *do* this, Charlotte,' Fleur implored her.

'I should have done it years ago. I've had an unfortunate life.'

'But what about the rest of us?' Fleur tried to appeal to her.

'You don't need me at all. I have no role to play.'

'We all care about you, Charlotte,' Fleur said quietly. 'If you must go away, why not just take a holiday? The weather is perfect. You could go up to the islands, anywhere you liked.'

'I'm going to Kurt.'

Fleur permitted herself a shocked gasp. 'You can't do that!'

'Why ever not?' Charlotte asked harshly. 'Plenty of your generation do it.'

'It seems pretty foolishly romantic, don't you

think? You've always set such a good example.'

'And it's written all over me. I'm an old maid, a lost soul.'

'What's so clever about being married? Or living with someone? Does living alone make you less of a person?'

'*Yes*,' said Charlotte with a whole lot of feeling. 'Kurt cares about me, I know.'

'Don't go to him, all the same,' Fleur warned. 'In the first place you'd shock him out of his mind. He sees you as a goddess, and it's difficult for goddesses to get off their pedestal. Again, he's very conscious of doing the right thing himself. It would be a mistake, Charlotte, I *know*.'

Charlotte ceased packing and sat on the bed. 'Does he really see me as a goddess?'

'His very words,' Fleur assured her earnestly. 'How do you think he'd feel if you arrived on his doorstep with a nightie and a toothbrush?'

'It is pretty laughable,' Charlotte admitted, but she looked very sad.

'All right, what you do,' said Fleur, 'is not revolt at all, not so anyone would notice. You plan. I think of you as a great planner—look how you arrange the parties! You can even loosen up a little with Kurt—the human touch. Ring him up and ask him about a book or something. If you think things are moving too slowly, ask him out. I can tell you it's deep and serious with him, but he's a little worried about your money.'

'Not *again*!' groaned Charlotte, sick to the heart. 'It's more difficult to have money than not to have it at all. It has, I've found, an identity of its own. I've been wooed for my fortune, which incidentally I suppose Grandfather *has* provided, now I'm about to be rejected for the same thing.'

'How much have you got?' Fleur asked helpfully without the slightest curiosity.

'Millions, I guess. The cheques keep coming in.'

'Would you consider giving it away?'

'I would *not*!' Charlotte answered sharply. 'In the first place I can't, in the second place I'm not so splendidly romantic that I think anything lasts. Kurt might think quite differently of me once we were married.'

'If anything I think he would feel more.'

'All right,' Charlotte sighed. 'What do you advise me to do?'

They sat talking for ages until finally Matthew tapped on the door. 'Isn't anyone going to *eat* around this house?'

It was a source of great satisfaction to both women that Matthew's appetite had picked up enormously, so his plaintive cry was like a call to arms. 'Thank God Grandfather has gone out,' said Charlotte, and got up off the bed.

CHAPTER EIGHT

FOR the entire holiday period Matthew kept well and happy, then the day before he was due to go back to school he started to wheeze.

'Oh, where's that damned ventilator!' Charlotte in her anxiety smashed a bottle of mouthwash on the bathroom floor. 'Look at *that*!' she exclaimed exasperatedly.

'I'll fix it,' offered Fleur.

'No, you go back to him,' Charlotte put her hand on the ventilator at last. 'To think this had to happen, and he's been so blessedly well.'

'I *hate* school,' Matthew confided after his second puff.

'Why? You're so clever.' Fleur was dismayed by the pallor of his skin. White under tan made for a curious green.

'It's a bore.'

'It's what we make of things, Matthew, that counts. School doesn't have to be boring unless you approach it with that attitude of mind. It's what's known as being negative.'

'You don't really think I'm that?' Matthew rasped.

'I think you have it in you to make us all very proud.'

'I don't want to be an engineer,' Matthew said

doggedly.

'You don't have to think about it yet.' Fleur took his hand. It was faintly trembling from the drug.

'But I *do*. Grandfather's such a difficult man to live with.'

'He's all right.' Handled the right way, he was. 'Anyway, I give you my solemn word you'll be what you want to be. If you want to be an architect, that's *it!*'

'Anyway, he might be dead.'

Fleur was shocked. 'Heavens, Matt, what a terrible thing to say!'

'Yes, I'm sorry. He's so much nicer since you've been here. Everyone and everything is so much nicer. I don't want to go to school at all. I want to stay home.'

'Well, you can't, and that's final.' She slapped his hand. 'I'm going to drive you in the morning and I'm going to pick you up in the afternoon and you're going to tell me all that's happened in between.'

'Will you really?' Matthew looked pathetically grateful. 'I can go in the bus.'

'The car needs running,' she told him in a matter-of-fact voice. 'Besides, it would be a pleasure.'

By nightfall the wheeze was gone, but Julian didn't seem at all pleased with Fleur's plan.

'You *can't* become the boy's crutch,' he told her firmly.

They were inside the study and the door was

shut.

'Won't you simply *listen*? He needs me.'

'I'm aware of that, Fleur.' He sounded as though he didn't think it any good thing.

The ring of the phone whirred into the silence and he picked it up. 'Standford,' he said, short and very formidable. 'Oh, how are you?' A slightly warmer tone, but not the least encouraging. 'No, I'm sorry, she's not at home ... yes, I will. ... Goodbye.'

'Who was that?' Fleur looked straight at him suspiciously.

'No one.'

'I think it was someone for me.'

'It can't be helped. You're not at home.'

She was struck dumb by his tyranny. He was just the kind of man to act first and ask later—if he ever bothered to ask at all.

'Next time Sheena rings, I'll tell her you're not at home,' she snapped.

'O.K. with me.' He stepped around the desk and leaned against it. 'You can't make Matthew too dependent on you, Fleur. I think it would be better if he went to and fro on the bus.'

'Too late now. I've already promised him.'

'You *can* see that you're becoming overly important to him.'

'It's a natural reaction.' She hung her head. 'Just give him a little time. He's not used to having me home yet.'

'Who *is*?'

They were on shaky ground now, so she decided

to stand up. 'Please let me take him for a while, Julian, just to ease him in. I think he fears if he turns his back I'll go away again.' She gave him an appealing look.

'You know I'm not going to let that happen.' His eyes travelled over her face and throat, and so great was their impact she shivered.

'Who was it really on the phone?' she asked.

'Run along,' he said, quite equably.

'You brute!'

'Stay then if you like,' he said softly. 'This room can be our refuge. I'll lock the windows and doors.'

'All I'd need to do is scream.' Despite the bravado in her voice she backed hurriedly to the door.

'You haven't been doing much of that lately.' His blue eyes sparkled like the sun on water.

'Oh well, I'm becoming quite used to being made love to.'

It was an outrageous lie, but it made her feel quite happy as she slipped out of the room.

With Matthew off to school, the routine changed. Julian went away again and Fleur began to think seriously what she should do in life. She had always wanted to go on to university, and now she had the money to do it. She would become a high school teacher. The teaching profession had always appealed to her.

Jon, when she told him, burst into tolerant, chauvinistic laughter. 'But, little girl, you were born to get married.'

'I was born to improve my mind. And go on improving it,' she retorted, incensed. Dictator or no, Julian was all for upgrading the status of women. He had even told her she had better think about enrolling.

So she did. Fleur's real nature, though buoyant and vivacious, was far from being frivolous. She had to have a purpose in life. She had to accomplish something—for herself, for others. She was going to be a teacher, a good one.

The weeks slipped away and because Fleur wasn't home for much of the day, she didn't realise Charlotte wasn't either. These days Charlotte was looking much more relaxed and womanly, so it didn't come as any great surprise when she announced that she was going to become an Easter bride.

'God in heaven!' Sir Charles spoke up without the slightest hesitation. 'Not the gardener feller?'

'Indeed, yes!' Charlotte, for once, wasn't at all affected. 'I wear his ring.'

'I don't suppose we can see it?' Sir Charles asked waspishly.

'You can.' Charlotte took it out of her pocket and put it on her hand.

'Every happiness, my dear.' Julian lifted his wine glass.

'I can't see how he paid for it.' Sir Charles leaned across the table. It was a remarkably fine stone, a sapphire surrounded by diamonds.

'May I see?' Fleur jumped up and ran around the table.

'Ah, the accomplice!' said Sir Charles dryly.

'It's beautiful, Lottie. Really beautiful!' Fleur kissed the older woman on the cheek.

'So you're going to think about getting married in your forties?' the old man asked.

'I'm thirty-eight, Grandfather, as you very well know.'

'You have to excuse me for forgetting a couple of years,' he grunted.

'I think we'd better have Kurt to dinner, don't you?' Julian spoke to Fleur more than to anyone else.

'*I* shan't be here.' Sir Charles seemed determined on starting something.

'Oh yes, you will!' Julian looked at the old man and away again. 'We Standfords stick together. Of course, Lottie, you'll be married from the house?'

Charlotte waited for her grandfather to speak, but he didn't, so she blushed and said, 'That would be lovely.'

'You could find someone twice as good if you tried,' Sir Charles nibbled furiously on his lip.

'You'll have reason yet to be proud of Kurt, Grandfather. He's only been in this country a short time, yet already he has a very successful business and great plans to expand.'

'No doubt with the help of your money.'

'I don't think he's particularly interested in it,' said Julian. 'In fact, Grandfather, in that respect he's beyond criticism.'

'He must be mad!' Sir Charles stood up stiffly. 'Marry him if you must, but don't ever say I didn't warn you.'

Charlotte's wedding turned out to be a grand social occasion. Of course there were people there who were quite insincere in their smiles and congratulations, but for the most part everyone wished Charlotte and her new husband a lifetime of happiness. At least there would be enough money to cushion the blows, and Charlotte looked radiant. To love and be loved is the greatest blessing on earth, and its effect on Charlotte was a revelation. No one had ever seen her in better looks, nor heard her so mellow-tongued.

Before they drove away, she kissed Fleur, her only attendant, emotionally. 'Thank you for everything. I'd never have found the courage but for you.'

'I will add my thanks to that.' Kurt, too, kissed her. 'It seems to me, little Fleur, you stage-managed the whole affair, and I am very, very happy.'

No one seemed to want to leave Waverley. The catering was superb and there was plenty more left to drink.

Sheena found Fleur momentarily alone and pulled her down beside her on the sofa.

'A perfect day! Didn't Lottie look a picture? Of course she's really good-looking, but until recently she didn't seem to know how to make the most of herself.'

'She does now,' Fleur was still smiling dreamily, misty-eyed. 'I shouldn't be surprised if she blossomed into a stunning woman. She's never really found herself until now, nor even known her own type.'

'It's common knowledge you had a hand in the match,' commented Sheena.

'Not really!' A little acid was dribbling through Sheena's pleasant manner and finally Fleur heard it. 'I like Kurt. I'm sure he'll make Charlotte very happy.'

'But goodness, dear, for a *Standford*?'

'What exactly do you mean?' Fleur turned her titian head right around to look at her.

'How could anyone take him seriously?'

'I never knew you were such a terrible snob,' said Fleur coldly.

'Oh, I am!' Sheena shrugged a silk-clad shoulder. 'Of course, you weren't born into a privileged background.'

'That was probably a good thing,' Fleur said tartly.

It wasn't the response Sheena wanted, so she started again. 'You never mention your father?'

'I never knew my father,' Fleur said.

'Poor thing!'

'Why don't you come to the point?' Fleur challenged her. 'You're obviously trying to tell me something—not pleasant, I'm sure.'

'You're not illegitimate,' Sheena laughed reassuringly.

'I wouldn't care if I were!' Fleur inhaled deeply. 'It's only people like you who make the less fortunate cringe.'

'Little bitch!' Sheena's dark eyes flashed. 'You mightn't look like your femme fatale mother, but I do believe you could cause the same amount of trouble.'

'You know *nothing* of my mother!' Fleur said icily, and went to stand up.

'I know she was madly in love with Julian, only David saw her first.'

She didn't have to wait long for this to take effect. Fleur's legs buckled under her. 'What are you saying?'

'What everyone knows. Your mother married one brother while she was crazy about the other.'

'But she was years older.' Fleur's green eyes looked dazed.

'What, a handful? What does that matter? If one can believe what one's told she was incredibly beautiful and seductive, and she caused so much trouble! Lottie had her boy-friend taken off her. David, to a lot of people's minds, killed himself and she tormented the young Julian no end. Finally she had to go—there was no other way. Needless to say, with a pay-out.'

'I don't believe this,' Fleur murmured.

'Are you O.K.?' Sheena cast her a sharp look. Fleur had gone whiter than white. 'Who could blame you if you were shocked? You're in love with Julian yourself.'

'And you wanted to warn me?' Fleur gave an odd little smile.

'I'm concerned for you,' Sheena corrected. 'I mean, it just wouldn't do, would it, and you'd only get hurt. He must loathe the memory of your mother.'

'I thought you said he loved her.'

'Oh, he did.' Sheena picked up the advantage

quickly. She had never said that at all, nor thought it, but so much the better.

'How terrible!' muttered Fleur.

'Not very pleasant,' Sheena agreed. 'I didn't want to be the one to tell you, but you were certain to hear it some time.'

'Uncle David never took his own life,' Fleur said in a deadly quiet voice. 'And if you ever spread that rumour or cause it to come to my brother's ears I promise you I'll find a way to make you very, very sorry.'

'How?' Despite herself Sheena felt chilled by the seriousness of the younger girl's expression.

'Your father's business, I understand, depends almost directly on Standford good will. My brother is a Standford even if I'm not.'

'Why, I'd never, *ever*. . . .' So presented, Sheena was lost for words.

'How are the mighty fallen!' said Fleur, looking as though she were about to faint.

Nothing was the same after that. She couldn't be alone with Julian for an instant. It was as she had always been told; Julian was the cause of her mother's eternal misery and her expulsion from the house. It must have been a terrible situation, not new but shameful, a triangle that could and did end in tragedy.

All that there was to gratify her, and it was a great deal, was the beautiful and touching serenity Matthew was achieving in his daily life. Urged on by Fleur's own study habits, he did extremely well in the end-of-term exams and though he would never be an athlete, a continued swimming programme had brought him to a peak of physical fitness he had never achieved before. These days he walked with his shoulders held back and the development of his torso was clearly visible. Fleur never watched him without a lump in her throat, but mindful of Julian's warning she encouraged him to bring home his friends and make more. Waverley was ideal for entertaining and the youngsters loved the pool and the tennis court and the billiard room and Maria's informal barbecues when they were given the responsibility for cooking the steaks and sausages and rissoles for the hamburgers. It all worked out so immensely enjoyable, Sir Charles himself had taken to joining in.

'The improvement in that boy is remarkable,' he told Fleur. Matthew was sitting with his friends, hungrily hoeing into a feast. 'I've never seemed to be able to *enjoy* him until now. He's always been such a quiet, self-effacing child. Like David, of course. Thank God there was Julian to take my place. I've been waiting on a phone call from him all morning.'

Julian was on another business trip and it wasn't until the end of the month that he came home. At least the hectic life he led let Fleur forget him for whole minutes at a time. She would never accept what he had done, never forgive or forget it.

Her friendship with several young men continued and she also made many friends of her own sex. She had lived such a lonely life—her mother had never permitted anyone to come to the house—now all that had changed. Waverley was continually full of young people, and if anyone had thought Sir Charles would object they had badly miscalculated. He enjoyed young people enormously, their energy and enthusiasm and their easygoing approach to him made a nice change from a lifetime of deference and servility in business. One young friend of Matthew's had even called him Granddad, but, while Fleur and Matthew had held their breath he had only said comfortably:

'Sir Charles to you, young feller.'

Jon Talbot still kept up his determined courtship even though Fleur had told him she had no intention of becoming serious about anyone. He seemed to accept it until inevitably he lost control.

They were on their way home from a party, but instead of driving straight to Waverley, he sought a secluded spot where he could at least kiss her.

'When is Standford coming home?' he asked abruptly. Julian was in Japan.

'Why?' Fleur looked away from the moon shimmering on the river and towards his darkened face.

'I want to know. What's between you two?'

'What the devil has it got to do with you?' Unexpectedly his question made her blaze into anger.

'A lot,' he said determinedly. 'I'm in love with you, Fleur.'

'So I don't see what that has to do with Julian.'

'No?' He put out a hand and kept her small, creamy face turned to him.

'*No!*'

'I think you love him—hate him. What does it matter? Such extremes in your case seem pretty close together.'

'You're mad!' she gasped.

'You can confide in me, you know.' He let her chin go, fully aware that he had upset her, but it was necessary. 'I've seen you both together. I've seen the way you look at him, the hurt and the anger mingled up with longing. You don't think I like it, do you? I want you for my own.'

'But I've *told* you, Jon. . . .'

'Faint heart never won fair lady.' He dropped his hand on to her shoulder. 'I know you want time, but I'm prepared to wait. Besides, if you've got a crush on Standford I feel the need to give you a sympathetic ear and a strong word of advice. He's already spoken for—I don't need to mention the lady's name. Personally I think they were made for each other. That kind of life would destroy a sensitive little creature like you.'

'Your warning really isn't necessary, Jon,' she said, too quietly.

'I'm glad, sweetheart. He's simply not worth it.' He glanced at her downbent head and pure profile. 'Do you realise what life would be like with a man like that? Why, he's never home and he's so damned attractive a woman would forever be left wondering if he was having affairs all over the world.'

'You don't know Julian,' she said. 'He's a very disciplined man, not the sort to litter his life with involvements. Women tend to cling and he would want to be rid of them. His real joy in life is business—not the money it brings in, but the excitement of big business itself. He's also tremendously far-sighted. Visions of the future fill his life. You don't know him at all.'

Jon didn't answer but stared thoughtfully ahead. He couldn't face losing her, yet every intuition told him she was breaking her heart over Standford.

'It's getting late, Jon,' she said gently. 'Shall we go?'

Normally he would have said, of course, but a pent-up frustration disturbed his normal calm.

'Why do you come out with me, Fleur?' he asked accusingly.

'Because I like you.' She looked at him uncertainly.

'I see.' He gave a savage little laugh. 'You go out with others, of course.'

'Yes, I do.' Her green eyes watched him closely, aware of his change in mood.

'Do you allow them to kiss you, caress you?'

'Oh, heavens, Jon!' she sighed crossly.

'Why don't you answer?'

Her laugh held a decided edge of tension. 'Actually, Jon, I'm not answerable to you for anything.'

'No, you just use me.'

'Damn it, that's not fair!'

'Who's to say?' he asked a little bitterly. 'Has Standford ever kissed you, held you in his arms?'

'I honestly don't remember!' The colour surged into her creamy skin, and Jon suddenly leant forward and switched on the interior light.

'*Ah!*' he said as though he was making a very specific diagnosis. 'You must take me for an awful fool.'

'I took you for a friend,' she said tonelessly, and looked away. 'Please let's go home, Jon.'

His face contorted in an angry, jealous grimace. 'How did you react when he kissed you? Like the cool little virgin I've always found you?'

'My God!' she muttered in disgust, and shook her shining head.

It was too much for Jon. He jerked her sharply towards him and pressed his mouth down hard on her own. It was a grinding kiss and she felt her bottom lip spurt with blood.

When he finally let her go, she drew a jagged little breath and touched her fingertip to her aching mouth. She drew it away and there was a smear of blood on her finger.

'God, I'm sorry!' There was a stunning change in Jon. He turned from brutal lover to the concerned medical man. 'Here, let me.' He took out a freshly laundered handkerchief and dabbed it to her mouth. 'Forgive me, Fleur. It was inexcusable of me.'

Her small face looked curiously unmoved, enigmatic. 'It might be best, Jon, if we don't see one another again. I do like you and I want you for a friend, but I can offer nothing more.'

'Yes, you can!' he said briefly. It was his opinion she could do with a little counselling, and he knew just the man. 'I'll ring you later on in the week. I feel so deeply about you, I suppose you find it hard to understand. I promise I'll never hurt you again, but you must allow me to keep on seeing you.'

She didn't answer, so he started up the car. No

woman was truly frigid. He just knew he could bring her alive.

Somehow they were home and she said goodnight and ran away up the steps. The lamps were still on in the garden and the exterior wall brackets on either side of the front door. She let herself in quietly and touched the switches that controlled the outside lights. They were always left on until the last member of the household was home.

There was no sound from within the big house, yet Fleur had the startled notion that someone was watching her.

'Matthew?' she called his name softly. Occasionally he waited for her to get home when he considered it was too late for her to be still out.

'Well, well, if it isn't Cinderella returning!'

She froze, and Julian moved out into the hallway, his comprehensive glance taking her in from head to toe.

He did this, appeared like the devil when one least expected him. 'You frightened me,' she said in a poignant little voice.

'Why?' His cool stare hardened and abruptly he turned on the overhead light. It was a magnificent twelve-light chandelier and it spilt its brilliance all over her.

'Good God!' he muttered with soft violence.

Fleur was very pale, her emerald eyes dilated and the injury to her mouth apparent in the faint swelling and the speck of congealed blood.

She could have sunk to the floor and died, instead she tilted her chin aggressively. 'You've done worse!' She was shivering in her thin dress though the night was far from cold.

A dangerous light flickered in his eyes and he advanced on her like a panther with such grace and co-ordination she was too fascinated to panic. 'The hell I have!' he said forcibly, and lifted her face to him. 'Now isn't this a tiny bit disgusting for a doctor?'

'He didn't mean it.' She was trembling, afraid of being so close to him again.

'I'd better deal with him, I think.' He looked extremely ruthless and her heart gave a great lunge of fright.

'I told you he didn't mean it. I provoked him unwittingly.'

Julian seemed to be holding himself under a steely restraint, the muscles of his face taut, a pulse throbbing in his temple. 'It seems to me, Fleur, you're too damned provocative by far. Next time he'd do a better job—only there's not going to be a next time.'

She drew in her breath but didn't dare pull away. 'Don't try to interfere in my life,' she said urgently. 'I can handle Jon.'

Anger flashed in his eyes. 'It's his attempt to handle *you* I don't like.'

She was instantly overwhelmed by the impossibility of it all; her own inexorcisable feelings and Julian's betrayal. How brutal life was, that she should be tied to him, an irrevocable bond neither of them could pretend to break.

Though it was the last thing she wanted, she was so much off balance she started to cry, heartbreaking little sobs that spoke of the enormity of her involvement.

'Don't *do* that,' he said harshly, as though her helpless femininity was too terrible to be borne.

'You don't really think I want to?' She looked up at him in a frenzy, her green eyes full of tears.

Julian muttered some fervent exclamation and swung her high in his arms. 'What am I going to do with you, Fleur?'

'God knows.' She turned her face into his throat. She simply couldn't cope any more. The sight of him sent such a physical pain through her body. She had evaded him for weeks and tortured herself with the old ghastly stories, but such was his hold on her there was nothing in the world for her but his nearness and immense strength. She shut her eyes tightly and relaxed in his arms, an emotional reaction from exhaustion and strain.

'You're not going to sleep, are you?' His voice came to her from a haze and this time it sounded incredibly gentle.

'Only for a moment. I'm so tired.' She tightened her arms around his neck.

'Who could blame the poor devil?' said Julian tightly.

She was being carried somewhere, but she didn't care. Her life was one long pretence, a great battle against Julian. 'St .. a .. y with me,' she whispered, slurring her words now.

'Bravely spoken, flower-face.' He wasn't in the least shocked.

She felt terribly lightheaded, her limbs made of

cotton wool. The next moment she felt the softness of a bed beneath her, the scent of sunlight and roses. She opened her eyes and glanced upwards instinctively.

Julian was bending over her, the dull golden gleam from the table lamp falling over the side of his face. His brilliant eyes were crystal clear, but their expression inscrutable.

'It's almost two o'clock,' he said quietly, and touched his fingertips to her cheek.

'I won't see Jon again.' She found herself promising him as though he controlled her.

'Tonight proved that, didn't it?' His eyes dropped to her sweet, vulnerable mouth.

'He's good really—kind and reliable and honest.' There was a note of ineffable sadness in her voice.

'All the things you think I'm not.'

'We know too much about each other, Julian,' she said, and sighed painfully.

'Forgive me, but you don't know me at all.' A flicker of bitterness surged into his voice.

'And shall *never* know,' she whispered as though it was a sacred vow. 'It never takes us long to quarrel, does it?' She drew a deep, anguished breath. 'I would go only Matthew needs me.'

'Are you sure?'

'That Matthew needs me?' She gave him a frightened, confused look.

'That you'd go.' His voice had the cynical note that always made her feel crushed.

'You like to hurt me, don't you?' She turned her

golden-red head lest he see the glitter of tears.

'Are you sure I'm the only one to do that? You've been treating me like a leper for months.'

'To preserve my soul,' she said clearly. 'Sheena told me everything.'

'Surely you could survive it,' Julian replied with mocking arrogance. 'There've been other women besides Sheena—quite a few. Nothing desperately wicked about it.'

'Oh, *God*!' she sighed in such a wretched voice, he put out his hands and held her tightly by the shoulders.

'What else did you talk about?' he demanded.

'Things I never wanted to know.'

'*Tell* me!' He shook her.

'It never ever occurred to me—*never*.'

'Fleur!' His hands tightened to pain.

'She told me,' she brokenly, 'you were passion-ately in love with my mother.'

'And you believed her, considering she was no-where around at the time?'

'A lot of people knew of your dangerous love. One of them was waiting to tell me.'

'You little fool!' His voice was empty of all emo-tion. Empty and drained.

'You don't deny it?' She was pleading with him for a full confession, a willingness to do penance.

'Why should I?' His handsome face hardened into an imperious cast. 'My life's work is based on trust—trust and respect. Once you were living and full of faith.'

'I was barely twelve at the time!' she exclaimed.

He put his fingertips against her mouth to forestall any argument. 'It's strange to think though Helena is dead she can still wreck lives,' he said harshly.

'Don't, Julian. Don't let's discuss it,' she said with a sudden sickening. Her mother had been a selfish, clinging, neurotic woman, but she had been her mother all the same.

'I suppose Sheena also told you my brother ran his car deliberately into a tree?'

Fleur turned her head away and he caught her chin. '*Answer* me,' he said with hard authority.

'I never believed it.'

'She has been busy!' Julian's mouth twisted in a grimace of contempt. 'David might have been very unhappy, but he would never have sacrificed his son's happiness. Besides, he had too much quiet strength. It was an accident. We were all very sure of it, even Helena, who lived to drive people to the brink.'

'Then why did you love her?' She sat up very quickly, thinking she was shouting.

'I despised her,' he said coldly.

'As I despise *you*?' She was mad with confusion, careless he might strike her.

Instead he stood up as though the less he had to do with her the better.

'I'm sorry, Julian.' She almost recoiled from the expression on his face. 'Please try to understand how I feel.'

'Whatever for?' His brilliant eyes moved over her with cold indifference. 'Maybe the doctor will suit you after all. All you ever seem to need is comfort.'

She couldn't argue with that; she was in no fit

state to. He walked away to the door and a little later she dragged herself off the bed. Her face in the bathroom mirror looked pale and tragic. She lifted a hand and touched the little sore spot on her mouth. She felt drunk with misery and exhaustion, yet she turned away and ran the shower. It was impossible to go to bed without washing away the effects of the night.

CHAPTER NINE

CHARLOTTE and Kurt were away for six months and immediately they got home Charlotte confided her news.

They were seated on the sun-porch of Charlotte and Kurt's new home with Matthew and the collies clearly visible to them through the huge picture window.

'I'm pregnant, Fleur,' Charlotte said gruffly, and pushed Fleur's coffee towards her so hurriedly some of the liquid spilt into the saucer.

'But that's wonderful news!' Fleur's face lit up with pleasure.

'Do you really think so?' said Charlotte.

'Don't you?' Fleur looked up into Charlotte's face. It was suffused with colour and plainly agitated.

'I don't know. I don't know what to think,' Charlotte confessed. 'I know I sound like a fool, but I never thought it would happen.'

'Why ever not?' Fleur looked her astonishment.

'My age,' said Charlotte, and sat down heavily. It was true she had put on weight, but it was extremely becoming and gave her a much softer, womanly image.

'But you're still a young woman.'

'Too old to have a baby.'

'Plenty of women have babies at your age.' Because Charlotte didn't seem capable, Fleur poured the tea and set it down carefully in front of the older woman. 'Drink up.'

'Thanks.' Charlotte stared down at the teacup. 'I feel as if I'm in the worst quandary of my life. Since I found out I scarcely know what I'm doing.'

'I imagine lots of women feel overcome when they start a new life,' Fleur offered soothingly. 'How does Kurt feel?'

Charlotte's blush deepened. 'He's thrilled, dazzled by the news. I've never seen him so happy.'

'Nor I.' Fleur caught hold of Charlotte's hand and squeezed it hard. 'You'll come through this beautifully, Charlotte—and think what it will mean to you both to have a child.'

'If only I weren't so *old*!' Charlotte moaned. 'It's not a good time of life to have a first baby.'

'Gosh, you're not *that* old,' Fleur said firmly. 'You have a good doctor?'

'The best.'

'Then let him do the worrying. You enjoy yourself. You're not sick or anything, are you?'

'Extraordinarily enough, no.' Charlotte began to drink her tea. 'A tiny bit queasy in the morning, but Kurt waits on me hand and foot. Honestly, you'd think I was the most precious little thing in the world instead of a big, tall woman.'

'I've never seen you look better,' Fleur said softly, and waved to Matthew through the window. 'You know yourself how you've blossomed. I think it's wonderful news, Charlotte.

You're a very lucky woman.'

'I am at that!' Charlotte agreed, the brilliance in her eyes leaving Fleur in no doubt. 'I'm tall too, which is good when one is carrying a baby. How do you think Grandfather will take the news? I'm almost too embarrassed to tell him.'

'Don't be,' said Fleur. 'Tell him with pride.'

It was a nine-day wonder Julian and Sheena had broken up, and even more of a wonder when she wasn't replaced. Though Julian was far from being a playboy, at thirty-four, he had had a stream of glamorous women in his life. Now, to the society crowd's consternation, there were none. Some said he was having a bad time recovering from Sheena, others laughed that to scorn, but none seemed able to accept that he wasn't paying any attention to the dozen or so young women who were doing everything in their power to attract him short of leaping beneath his car. And even this had been discussed. It was unthinkable that a wealthy bachelor should be allowed to go free, and when he was devastatingly handsome a shocking reflection on the women themselves. Gossip raged and plans were made, and Sheena, to no one's surprise, flew quietly out of the country. She might have let one rich man slip through her fingers, but it was certain in Europe she would pick up another.

'I'm glad Sheena's gone,' Matthew told Fleur confidentially. 'She was good-looking, I guess, but not half good enough for Uncle Julian. Boy, wasn't she huffy the last time we saw her!'

'Revolting,' agreed Fleur. Sheena had spotted them at a shopping centre and when Matthew had turned away she managed to let Fleur know exactly what she thought of her.

'Do you mind if we have Stephen over for the weekend?' Matthew asked idly—more a courtesy than anything else.

'Of course not.' Fleur put another disc on the record player. 'He's a very interesting boy.'

'He hopes to make a mark in the world of big business. I shouldn't be surprised if he comes to Uncle Julian for a job. And speaking of Uncle Julian,' Matthew added too casually, 'what's wrong between the two of you?'

'Nothing,' Fleur said firmly.

'Well, if you *won't* tell me——' Matthew answered with calm.

'I suppose I ought to,' Fleur murmured, hurting inside. 'As a matter of fact I might have to. . . .'

'I suppose you're in love with him?' Matthew roused himself off the floor to ask.

'Now why should you think that?' Fleur caught her breath. Though she was supposed to be the one full of grief and grievances it was Julian who was acting totally disgusted.

'I may be just a simple kid,' Matthew said cheerfully, 'but I'm not stupid. Actually I think there's no better man in the world for you.'

'You can be sure Julian thinks differently.' Fleur got out of her armchair, restlessly. 'What about taking the dogs for a walk?'

'Sure thing!' Matthew hopped up agreeably. 'I

suppose you know Sholto ate half the paper this morning. Grandfather was furious!'

'Oh, I don't think so,' Fleur said mildly. 'He just likes to make a lot of noise.' In actual fact Sir Charles loved the dogs and often let them sit on his feet. The occasional grumble was not to be taken seriously.

They were walking hand in hand down the front stairs when Julian pulled into the driveway.

'Oh, hi, Uncle Julian!' Matthew was delighted. He didn't see half enough of his uncle even at the weekend.

'Hi.' Julian got out of the car and ruffled the boy's hair. 'Where are you off to?'

'We were taking the dogs for a walk, but now that you're home. . . .' Matthew's hand slid into his uncle's and gripped. 'Can't we all do something together? I wish we could.'

Fleur had stopped dead beside the bank of camellias and Julian looked over Matthew's head towards her. 'How are you, Fleur?'

Common civility and just enough devastating mockery to make her defiant. 'Fine, thank you, Julian,' she answered with an air of cool calm.

'Well?' Matthew prompted them.

'As it happens,' said Julian, 'I have the afternoon free. Or I'm going to take the time out. What would you like to do?'

'Fleur?' Matthew looked to his sister for a suggestion.

What could she tell him—she didn't want to go? 'I'll leave it up to you.'

'Then why don't we take a run down the beach?'

suggested Matthew. 'I miss the coast, and we could take Sholto and Mac.'

'As I recall, one of them was sick the last time.' Julian leaned in the car and picked up his jacket.

'They're trained now,' said Matthew. 'That's what matters. They're quite used to the car. Fleur takes them everywhere.'

'In that case, they can go.' Julian shot Fleur a quick look, impossible to define. She was wearing jeans and a T-shirt, yet she still managed to look very feminine and fragile.

'What car are we taking?' Matthew asked.

'The best car on the road!' Julian patted the hood of the Double-Six with real affection. 'Come on, jump to it!'

Fleur behaved herself all the way down. So did the collies. Matthew was so excited and pleased he practically talked non-stop, so it wasn't terribly noticeable that Fleur and Julian had practically nothing to say to each other.

It was still a little too chilly to swim, so they walked for miles along the glistening white sand, the collies racing and chasing the seagulls in ecstasy. If this was a dog's life, they looked magnificently happy, particularly when whenever they stopped they were petted and patted and somehow given to understand that no human in their right mind would be without a dog or two.

As the afternoon shadows lengthened, a lone fisherman came out, and Matthew with his jeans rolled up struck up a conversation. He was much more outgoing now, taking his cue from Fleur, who was naturally friendly. To everyone except Julian and now they were alone.

'Here, put this under your head.' Julian rolled up his expensive sweater and put it behind her head.

'Thank you.' What else could she say?

He sat down beside her, his fingers slowly releasing handfuls of sand. 'You're turning into an awful bore, Fleur,' he told her.

'I know. I even bore myself.'

'Tell me what you've been doing all week?' He leaned over on one elbow and looked down at her, relaxed on the sand.

'Studying mostly.'

'You're a very serious student.' His eyes trapped her wavering glance.

'I'm aiming towards true self-sufficiency.'

'What a big yawn!'

'*I'm* trying, Julian,' she told him.

'How's your love life?' he asked next.

'Come to an end. I dislike unnecessary situations.'

'Still, you're out a lot these days.'

'I've taken on extra classes,' she explained.

'I see.'

'Let's change the subject,' she said. His blue eyes were making her lose her hard-won self-possession.

'Honestly, darling, I can't think of a thing.'

It had been ages, *ages*, since he had used the casual endearment, and she shivered. 'Too bad!'

'You look so tragic,' he said.

'I am *perfectly all right*.' She shut her eyes.

'If I lie down beside you what will happen?'

'You'll get sand in your hair.' She had been

almost relaxed, now she was very aware of her own body and the warm heat that was moving over her in waves. Being with Julian was like doing exquisite violence to herself. If she only moved a fraction, she could turn right into his arms. No one had ever held her like Julian, touched her so intimately. She had thought she had made herself strong, now he was peeling away every protective skin. She felt naked and vulnerable.

It was altogether very strange. Both of them lay quietly, thinking their own thoughts, and after a while Matthew ran back to them.

'He caught a fish. A beauty! What about if we get some fish and chips on the way home?'

When they eventually arrived back at Waverley it was dark and Julian drove straight into the garage.

'I'll get the dogs out,' said Matthew, and jumped out. 'They've been so good, but they'll be pleased to get out and have their dinner. Here, Sholto! Here, Mac!' The dogs scampered out of the back seat and dashed away. 'I don't want any dinner,' Matthew called, not surprisingly.

'All right.' Fleur smiled. She and Julian, apparently not hungry, had sat and watched him polish off two large pieces of ocean mullet and a great pile of chips.

She still had Julian's blue sweater tied around her neck and she slid out of the car and stretched. All that sea air had made her feel sleepy.

'Coming?' Julian called to her, his hand on the light switch.

'Ummm!' All at once she felt peculiar, excited and alarmed.

She heard Julian switch the light off and now she couldn't see.

'Julian?' Her voice shook.

He said dryly: 'Over here.'

'Couldn't you have waited until I got there?' She tried for a cool tone, only it wasn't coming out that way.

The next thing his hands were hard on her shoulders, his dark face above her. Her heart rocked crazily and she moved right into his arms, pressing herself against him, in the grip of an emotion so powerful she didn't even know how to protect herself.

'Kiss me, Julian,' she begged him, and offered him her mouth.

'I don't understand you, Fleur,' he sighed. 'I don't understand you at all.'

'But you *do*!' Her arms came up to encircle his neck and suddenly it was he who was crushing her, embracing her with an intensity that outstripped her own. It was astonishingly violent and passionate, but both of them seemed to welcome the pain.

Whatever Julian was, whatever he had done, she loved him. She couldn't alter it by the smallest part. *What is written, is written.* She remembered his words.

'You know I love you,' she said in a broken whisper, and lifted her head so he could kiss along her throat.

'Yes.' There was no mockery in his voice, but

the truth at last.

'Don't use it as a weapon. *Please*, Julian.'

'I'll beat you, Fleur!' He spoke with some violence.

'Whatever you want.' She covered his face with small, desperate kisses.

'Don't say that!' He grasped her head in his two hands. 'Remember who I am. Remember you think I made you suffer.'

'I only know I love you. I've loved you all my life.'

He seemed to give an agonised groan, then he covered her mouth again, kissing her with a dark, frightening passion he could never again deny. 'I want you,' he muttered blindly. 'I want you so much I can't even think straight.'

'But, darling' she teased his sculptured mouth with small kisses, 'Who's asking you to think?'

He seemed to catch his breath and his lean body went rigid.

'Would you come with me now?' His hand stilled on her breast.

'Yes. What else can I do?'

'It's your *mind* I want, Fleur,' he said in a furiously sincere voice. 'Not just your sweet, flawless body. I want your trust and your pride and your deep abiding affection. I guess I want everything.'

And that was the terrible part. Old griefs were stubborn, outlasting the fury of passion. Some could never be erased. Fleur sighed deeply and in an instant he became totally unreachable.

There were voices outside the garage; Charlotte's calling urgently: 'Julian, Fleur? Come quickly! Grandfather has had a stroke!'

CHAPTER TEN

It was already dark outside; Fleur had not realised it was so late. She got up off her bed and moved slowly through to the adjoining bathroom. She had an appalling headache.

The bright overhead light made her wince. She shook tablets out into her hand, then swallowed them down with a glass of water. She had never been sure of her real feelings towards Sir Charles Standford, but she was very, very sorry he was dead.

I must lie down again, until the tablets take effect, she thought. She moved back on her stockinged feet towards her bed. It had been a very large funeral, but just as terrible and chilling as her mother's less than a year before. At least the old man had gone quickly, when her mother had taken months to die.

As she reached the bed, she lurched forward and fell on it. All she wanted to do was forget; forget everything.

An hour passed, then there was a tap on her door.

'Fleur?' Charlotte came in very slowly, staring at the small figure on the bed.

'It's all right, Lottie, I'm awake.'

'We were worried about you.' Charlotte dragged herself into a chair. All her strength and vitality seemed quenched.

It was this more than anything that made Fleur pull herself together.

'Has everyone gone home?' she asked, and brought herself upright.

'Yes.' Charlotte's lips parted in a profound sigh. 'I can't believe he's dead.'

'It was just the way he would have wanted it,' Fleur told her.

'Julian. My God, Julian, what a burden he has to bear!' Charlotte lifted her hands, then put them over her face.

'Don't upset yourself, Charlotte,' Fleur begged. 'Especially not now. Julian is strong. You needn't be afraid for him.'

'Yes,' said Charlotte, 'he's an extraordinary man. I used to be jealous of his brilliance once, for David's sake. The ability he has to draw people to him; men and women. It never occurred to me that that left Julian very much alone. He was the youngest. Our parents were dead. I've always been very hard on Julian because he was somehow everything David and I were not. I blamed Julian for many things, his popularity and extra-ordinary talents, the way my grandparents idolised him—because they *did*. I even blamed him for what happened to David, though no one could have been less guilty.'

Charlotte's blue eyes had a bruised look and Fleur got up and came to her side. 'He couldn't have planned to love my mother,' she said.

'What?' Charlotte fought out of her exhaustion. 'What are you saying, child?'

'After all,' Fleur bit her lip, 'a lot of people seem to know.'

'Dear God!' Charlotte looked at the girl with compassionate eyes. 'Who has so unsettled you?'

'Sheena told me everything.' Fleur dashed the tears from her eyes.

'And she told you,' Charlotte said abruptly, 'Julian was in love with your *mother*?'

Fleur could not speak.

'My dearest child,' Charlotte stood up in her agitation, 'you've done violence to yourself all for nothing. Julian didn't care about Helena at all. At the beginning she was no more to him than the woman his brother had chosen. None of us were happy about it, but for the only time in his life, David held firm. He married his Helena and never had a minute's peace evermore. You see, dear— and I don't want to hurt you—Helena never loved David at all. She wanted security and position, freedom from money troubles. She used David like men are used every day. She hurt him dreadfully— especially when she made it plain she found his younger brother attractive. It was Julian's im- munity that urged her on.' Charlotte turned and saw Fleur's eyes fixed on her face, shadowed by lack of sleep yet intensely brilliant.

'You mean Sheena was lying?'

'For her own ends,' Charlotte looked back at her steadfastly. 'How could you have listened?'

'He didn't deny it,' said Fleur.

'Julian would be like that,' Charlotte shook her head. 'He would feel, no matter what, you owed him your trust.'

'But why, Charlotte?' Fleur's lips trembled.

'Because he loves you.' Charlotte moved suddenly and put her hand on Fleur's cheek.

'But surely he could have explained a little?'

'No.' Charlotte's smile twisted. 'One has to see behind Julian's façade—the handsomeness, the power and success. In a way, he's always been alone.'

'I don't think,' Fleur said miserably, 'I can ever make things come right.'

Charlotte held out her hand to her and said in a quiet voice: 'You can try.'

After Charlotte and Kurt had gone home and Matthew was tucked up in bed, Fleur went to stand in the open doorway of the library. She had changed out of her black dress into a green velvet housegown, but Julian didn't even look up at her. He was sitting at the big mahogany desk with his face in his hands.

'May I come in, Julian?' she asked gently, conscious that he was unutterably weary.

He straightened and made an obvious attempt at normality. 'Yes, Fleur. I'm sorry if I didn't notice you.'

'Are you all right?' she asked anxiously. There was a pallor under his deep tan and his face was set in lines of strain. 'Can I get you anything?'

'No, no, I'll be all right. It's been a terrible day.'

She went to the cabinet, poured out a Scotch, added a little water and handed it to him. 'Here, drink this.'

'Thank you. Don't look so worried, Fleur, I'm

all right.'

She shrugged and leaned forward to throw another log on the fire. 'I have to worry, Julian, because you're all I've got.' There was a long silence and she went to sit on the chesterfield tucking her feet under her. 'It's not exactly the right time to tell you—you've got so many other things on your mind—but I love you, Julian, and I'm very, very sorry I ever doubted you. I suppose I loved you so much I couldn't deal with what I thought of as your betrayal; I was too wrapped up in my own bitterness and grief. I hadn't thought things out. I know you probably don't want to hear, but I must tell you all the same, and beg you to forgive me.'

'I don't blame you,' he said in an odd voice. 'You're so very young and so many things conspired to accuse me. The head knows these things, but the heart wants so much more.'

She knew then she had lost him. 'I'll say goodnight,' she said very quickly, before her voice broke.

She had scarcely reached the door before he caught her and drew her back into the room. 'Didn't I tell you, Fleur, you could never run away?'

She gave a muffled little exclamation and he picked her up in his arms, walking back towards the chesterfield. 'My grandfather had a genuine fondness for you,' he said quietly. 'Only a week ago he told me he would think me a fool if I let you slip through my fingers.'

'I can't believe it.' Fleur shook her head.

'He knew perfectly well why I was acting so strangely.' Julian sat down, cradling her in his arms. 'Just stay with me here, *please*.' He pressed her head back against his shoulder, seeming to derive enormous comfort from their physical contact.

The grim tensions of the day melted away and Fleur spoke the words closest to her heart. 'I love you, Julian.'

He lowered his head and kissed her white temple. 'That's my baby.'

'I've been so terribly blind and stupid.'

'Hush!' He tightened his hold on her. 'No matter who tried to come between us, we're still here. *Together*. At first I loved you as the sweetest little girl child this family had ever produced, now I want you, *need* you as a lover, my joy, my other self, my dearest, closest friend. I really want you for my wife.'

He was speaking into her silky hair and she began to weep softly.

'What a terrible time to cry!' He tipped up her expressive face. 'Don't you want to marry me?'

'Nobody else.' Fleur's constant, loving heart was reflected in her green eyes. 'There never was and there never will be anyone but you.'

'*Fleur!*'

Such a torrent of tenderness and passion was in his voice, she closed her lovely eyes and offered him her mouth. She had waited so long to re-find him, now the long agony was over.

They faced the future together, which was all she would ever want.

THE DISTINCTIVE EMERALD

Julian lends his mother's emerald earrings and emerald necklace to Fleur, so that she may wear the jewels for the big party his family gives for her after her long absence. Let's take a closer look at the emerald and what it signifies; then you'll see that Julian's gesture perhaps meant a good deal more than it first appeared to!

A favorite jewel of Cleopatra, the distinctive emerald is an adornment cherished by women the world over today. Symbol of love, prosperity, kindness and goodness, this precious gem was long ago believed to have magical powers, particularly in the area of healing the sick; and probably it was the emerald's restful green hue that gave rise to the idea that just gazing at the gem was good for the eyes.

In Julian's case, it seemed that the emeralds he gave to Fleur were also good for love!